THE
BUCCANEER'S
DAUGHTER

DEL GARRETT

Del Garrett

Copyright © 2017
Del Garrett
Cover Courtesy of Pixabay
ISBN: ISBN-10: 0-692-85576-9
ISBN-13: 978-0-692-85576-8

Published by Raven's Inn Press
806 Rhoden Rd.
Judsonia, AR 72081

Dedication

This book is dedicated to my lovely wife, Dana, who, although not a pirate or buccaneer, has nevertheless stolen my heart. Her continuous support for my writing is inspiring, in itself. With her encouragement and belief in me, I strive to do better with each new attempt. Thank you, my love.

Chapter 1
A Thief in the Night

I looked deep into the dark brown eyes of the man who stood before me holding a pistol in his hand. His eyes were more threatening than the pistol, for they stared deeply into my soul.

I found myself growing weaker as he watched me—hungrily, I might add, like a fox with a trapped hen, knowing it had its prey and had all the time in the world to enjoy the kill.

"Is this what you want?" I asked, holding out my heart-shaped locket.

"Aye, that and more." He smiled. His thin golden-colored mustache curled upwards at the corners of his mouth. The deep tan of his skin and dark vermilion of his lips gave contrast to the row of perfectly white teeth, which gleamed even in my darkened chamber as he grinned at me…as if there had been a joke made and only this handsome stranger knew its punchline.

"Surely you would take only that which a lady might offer, and nothing more."

"Surely I would take whatever the lady has to offer; *everything* the lady has to offer." His grin widened.

"I beg of you, sir; please leave me my dignity."

Outside the window I could hear the approaching sound of boots upon cobblestone. My wild-eyed thief also heard the soldiers approaching.

"M'lady, it seems that I have much less time than I had hoped to enjoy your company."

He held up the necklace and smiled at the locket which he had opened and which he now kissed and closed, draping the chain over his head to hang around his own neck.

"I leave you now to wonder what the night might have held for the two of us."

With that, he brushed his lips across mine, then leaped to the windowsill and swung himself outward, landing in the flower garden two floors below. He landed quietly. The soft dirt in the flowerbed not only cushioned his fall, it quieted the sound his boots might have made on hard dirt.

As he crouched there, two of the Redcoats hurried by looking for him. I looked down from the window. He looked up and saw me watching him. For a moment his face showed concern that I might alert the soldiers. From the other side of the hedge a rough-looking officer with a saber in his hand looked up at me and shouted, "Miss, have you seen him?"

The thief squatted in the flowerbed, hidden from view except from my perch in the window. I looked at him briefly then stared at the officer and pointed in the direction the two previous soldiers had taken.

"He went that way," I lied, forcing a tremor of feigned fear in my voice.

"Thank ye, ma'am," the officer said and ushered his men onward in the direction I had pointed.

I looked again at the thief. He stood, smiled at me, doffed his high-plumed hat and made a grandiose bow. Replacing the hat on his head, he blew me a quick kiss and winked conspiratorially at me. He ducked through the thick hedge and made his way across the courtyard to the far wall. Climbing it as though he were a monkey boy, he reached the top, took one last look in my direction and was gone in the night.

"Oh, my!" I felt weak enough to drop. I made my way to my bed and sat down upon it just as Aunt Eller opened the door and rushed to me.

"Oh, my poor baby. Did he hurt you?"

"N—no, not really. All he did was take my necklace."

"Thank heaven that's all he had time to take."

"Aunt Eller!"

"Shush, child. You are no longer a little girl. Your body has developed enough for any man to want you as a lover. You must be careful how you act in front of men from now on. It is said this very same thief took more than a mere necklace from Lady Covington when he visited her in the night last week."

I giggled.

"But I never saw him before tonight. I'd never flirted with the man. And, as to Lady Covington, I never heard..."

The Buccaneer's Daughter

"Nor has Lord Covington, I assure you. But gossip flows from the servants like water from a spigot. She's a lady and out of respect for her the word will never be widespread, I assure you. But Lord Covington is so much older than she and this thief has gained quite a reputation with the ladies that I am sure Lord Covington is wondering what has put such a smile on his ladyship's face."

Just then there came a rapping upon my door and George, the manservant, stuck his head in.

"Lieutenant Carstairs, mum. He wishes to..."

The lieutenant pushed his way past the manservant and entered my room. He was the same officer that I had spoken to from my window. He addressed me in a cautious manner, taking time to form his words carefully and precisely. "I need to know, Lady Esther, if you are absolutely certain of which direction you pointed as to where the thief had escaped."

He stood there with a look of frustration on his face; his hands propped on his hips, his feet spread wide apart, his bushy eyebrows lowered and a deep flush covered his cheeks. His nostrils flared widely and wildly as he waited for an answer.

"Oh, sir. I am not sure, now. I approached the window to look for the thief and I heard someone running off in the direction I indicated. I thought it was him."

Clearly the lieutenant didn't believe me. He snorted loudly, wiped a hand down his face and looked away. It was one thing to question a lady of royal blood, quite another to challenge her openly without proof.

"Thank ye, miss. Sorry to have troubled ye again."

Lieutenant Carstairs bowed politely, turned and stormed out of my chambers. A moment later I heard him grumbling beneath my window.

I moved across the room while Aunt Eller chatted incessantly about the condition of living in a coastal town with so many thieves and killers about.

Looking out my window, I saw that one of the lieutenant's men had stepped through the hedgerow and was holding a lantern high above his head as he pointed out where the thief had landed and made his way through the hedge.

He and the lieutenant, followed by four soldiers with rifles, traced the thief's path from the house across the yard and to the point where he had disappeared over the wall.

I drew back from the window as the lieutenant looked back in my direction. Afraid of what he might say to Father, or to the magistrate, I resolved myself to act as frightened as the situation demanded.

I knew Father would be concerned only for my safety…and of course, my virginity…and that he would care less about the necklace. After all, he had purloined it himself from the neck of some other lady on one of his boardings of a French ship.

It was ballyhooed loudly around the celebration that followed that trip that the necklace was the last thing Father had taken from off the lady's body just before he took her greatest treasure. I had asked him what the men had meant by that, but he never told me.

"There are matters you will learn about as you grow older, my princess." What I did know was that we were buccaneers and to us such trinkets were spoils for the taking. In that sense, we had more in common with the night's thief than we did with the king's soldiers.

At the same time, we were tied to the throne by blood. Father was first cousin to the king, not part of the family that was in the king's favor, I'm afraid. We were somewhat outcasts through a dalliance Father had made early in life with a lady to whom the king, then a prince, had been courting. When the prince discovered one night that Father had 'plucked' the rose in the garden before the prince had been able to sample its fragrance for himself, a lifelong hatred began which still held to this day.

The result, even though Father was titled, was a denouncing by the prince when he became king. Father would not share in the fortunes of the realm so he had taken to the trade of robbing the Spanish and French ships of their treasures; taking their livestock, butchering it and cooking it right there on the docks, selling the meat to anyone, including the unknowing ship crews whence the stock had originally been claimed.

It was a wonderful life and Father became rich, but he never took me along on any of his journeys until I had reached my teen years. Had I been born a boy, I would have shared in his adventures much sooner, I am sure.

Nevertheless, I loved my life. Up until now, it had been filled with simple merriment with teas and gardening and watching Punch and Judy shows in the park.

I must admit that after tonight, though, my life would take on new meaning. It must, for the young thief had stolen more than just my necklace.

He had stolen a little girl's innocence—mentally, if not physically—and at seventeen, had opened my eyes to a new awakening. He was a beautiful man, a dangerous man, and a man of considerable experience with the ladies, according to Aunt Eller.

Would I ever see him again? I hoped so. For even with the danger he presented, there was something so charming about him that made my heart flutter each time I remembered those piercing dark eyes burning their way into my very soul.

I had thought about boys before, of course, but now I was thinking about being with a man. What would it be like to make love to him? I liked what I saw and had we been blessed with more time, I'm sure I would have willingly submitted myself to him.

I slept a fitful sleep, tossing among my bed sheets. I dreamed of the thief climbing through my window, bending low over my bed and warming my neck with his hot breath.

In my dream, I opened my eyes to see him smiling at me. He bent his head low over me and I felt the warmth of his lips on mine, felt the wetness of his tongue as he probed deeply past my lips and into my mouth, stabbing my own tongue with his.

I felt his hands on my shoulders holding me down, lowering themselves to my breasts, pulling the gown away to expose my nipples to the cool night air.

The sensation of them growing as he tweaked first one then the other, then the lowering of his head as he licked each nipple, causing them to grow even larger, then taking them into his mouth one at a time and pulling on them with his teeth. Gently, like the fox nuzzling at the hen, he took his time to sample the blood that boiled within my veins, controlling me with his lovemaking. I couldn't help myself. I moaned loudly and curled my legs upward into a fetal position, digging both my hands between my legs and pressing deeply in that moist place where I so ached for his touch.

Then it was over. The dream faded and along with it his face, his hands on my body, his warm body pressing against me, his hot breath on my neck. Everything, all gone.

The night closed in around me in total darkness. I awoke to sunlight coming through the window and to sheets moist with perspiration and a more concentrated pool of moisture in the center of the bed.

I first blushed my shame, then my delight that I had been made love to, even if only in my dream, for it meant what Aunt Eller had warned me about. I had become a woman.

Chapter 2
Down to the Docks

The day was sunny and fresh with the briny smell of fish just hauled in from the sea. The nets were full and fishermen scurried around the docks loading their catches live into crates. Young boys piled the crates onto carts they then pulled along the docks to the open-air markets where merchants gutted the catches and sold or traded them for other goods.

Swordfish, shark and occasional shellfish made their way to family tables by way of the tradesmen. Portsmouth by the bay was an exciting sight for a young girl such as me. But today was more exciting than most. I often visited the docks when my father's ship, *The Neptune,* was in port. I traveled today in the company of Aunt Eller and her son, Phillip Wingate, my cousin and a charmer with the ladies.

I suppose that ran in the family, because all the males seemed dashing and I cannot recall ever meeting any of them who were not well mannered or bold in their interchange with others.

Today I felt more attuned to the sights and sounds and the olfactory surges that assailed my nostrils. I took greater notice in the rippling of muscles among the men and some of the boys; more notice of their long curls dripping wetly across their bare shoulders and more notice of the particular aromas of their bodies. I marveled at how each male smelled of the sweat of their work, but how distinguishable each male's scent was as I brushed near them.

Some were older and had the smell of bitter onions exuding from their pores. The younger ones had a sweeter smell like wildflowers mixed with whale oil, which we burned in our lamps. Strong. Compelling. I found that with a little concentration I could focus on these aromas individually and exclude the salty smell of the sea or the fish that came from it.

Doing this, I closed my eyes to take in these hefty scents of manly odor and clumsily bumped into one of the fishermen.

"Oh, pardon me," I offered an apology.

He glared at me, but seeing that I was a young lady and no doubt noticing that I had worn a low-cut dress that gave ample view of my cleavage, he softened his scowl and muttered, "Tha's okay, missy. 'Ave a nice day."

Phillip came to my rescue and gently guided me back on course toward Father's ship.

"My, oh my, dear cousin. You are causing quite a ruckus today. I should say that every man here is in danger of hurting himself by not being able to concentrate on anything but your beauty."

"And would that include you, my cousin?"

"Tease me not, Esther. I still remember you running around naked in a wading pool, quacking like a duck."

"I still run around naked sometimes, Phillip. But I don't quack like a duck anymore."

"Maybe we should see for ourselves," he teased.

"Ah, but only my future husband will ever find that out," I returned.

We stopped in front of *The Neptune* and saw that the crew was taking on supplies. That meant Father was about to head to sea again. I was feeling disappointed. I had hoped he would spend more time at home during this visit. I understood that he needed to work hard to provide for us as he did, which was quite handsomely as I have already mentioned, but I sorely missed sitting with him in the evening by the fire and hearing him tell me of his adventures on the high seas.

Oh, how I wished I had been born a boy so that I might join him as he took booty from the French or fought the Spaniards. My trips with him had been merchant trips where he traded up and down the coast. I had never seen him take on a French or Spanish vessel.

Like many foolish youngsters I wanted to hear the roar of the cannons, to see my father's men board another vessel and put to the sword all who did not surrender then to drag out the captain's treasure chest and enjoy the spoils of war. Such a thought had lured many a young boy to danger and sometimes to his death. Father protected me by only taking me on safe journeys. I know that now, still…how do you control the urges of your youth? That, of course, is what parents are for. Father instructed me in his own way and protected me and, without a wife, entrusted my teachings about womanhood to his sister.

The Buccaneer's Daughter

We mounted the gangplank and stopped at the top to let the boatswain announce our presence. The crew kept working, but bowed slightly as we walked past them to Father's quarters. I heard mumblings and low-pitched laughter coming from some of the men.

Once, Phillip even turned toward some of them and gave them a cold stare, which instantly drove them to silence. Phillip's face was flushed as he grabbed my arm rather roughly and hastened our steps to Father's cabin.

"Phillip, Aunt Eller." Father beamed at them. "And my dear, sweet Esther, just look at you." Father did look, and seeing the low cut blouse I wore and my heavy breasts pushed inward so tightly there was a great crevice between them, his face lost some of its smile. He glanced at Esther, who dropped her eyes as he raised an eyebrow of disapproval.

"And what is this I hear of a thief daring to steal from my darling daughter?"

"Oh, Father. I was not afraid."

"I'm sure you weren't, my dear. Still, I have ordered extra security for the townhouse. If you should see this blighter on the street you must point him out immediately."

"To the king's men?"

"Yes, they may as well do something worthy of being stationed in our city, especially with the taxes we have to pay the king for their presence. Here, I have something for you." Father reached inside a small chest upon the table where he kept his maps and removed a necklace that glistened green and gold. "This is jade," he said. "It comes from the Orient. It shall replace the necklace taken by the thief."

"Oh, Father. It's beautiful."

Father placed the necklace around my neck as he stood behind me. Looking down, I'm sure he had an excellent view of the tops of my breasts and the deep crevice between them. He said nothing, of course, nor did I. He closed the clasp and moved around to my front so he could see it dangling there just above the start of my cleavage.

"You have become a woman," he said. "I blinked my eyes and you grew up. You will be eighteen in two weeks. I will miss watching you chase butterflies and making mud pies."

"Father, I do not chase butterflies; I catch them on my fingers when they wish to land there; and I haven't made mud pies since I was eight years old."

"And in those days I had no gray in my beard. I suppose it is time for you to take a suitor. We'll talk of that when I return from my trip."

"As you wish, Father."

I smiled at him, partly because he had acknowledged me as being ready for marriage for I had longed to take my place within the adult world, but also by the look in his eyes. My father was first of all my father, but any man looking at a young woman with the charms I was displaying had nothing but nature's call to blame for the way his eyes took in the sights of a woman's breasts, the inward curve of her waist, and the full roundness of her hips.

The Buccaneer's Daughter

Father looked at me for the first time as a woman of desire. Had I been anything else but his daughter I am sure he would have impressed himself upon me, for he had a lusty reputation for and among the women of Portsmouth. After my brief meeting with the robber the night before, and my new sexual awakening, I feared not that my father would act inappropriately with me. I knew that he would not, but I now appreciated the way he looked at me and I now understood that look better than before.

A noise outside the cabin took Father's attention away from our conversation. Phillip followed him as he opened the door. Aunt Eller pulled me back deeper inside the quarters, but I slipped from her grasp to see what was happening.

Father stepped forward between two seamen who were scuffling on deck. He grabbed them by their necks and pulled them apart. One seaman drew back and dropped his guard, but the other man slapped Father's arm away with one hand and drew his knife with the other, taking a swipe at Father and cutting the sleeve of his jacket.

The rest of the crew drew back. It was unheard of to attack the captain of a ship and certainly Father's reputation would have seemed to warrant more respect. The sailor showed no signs of pulling back. Instead, he lunged forward with his knife. Father's grasp was quick and strong and before the sailor could move again, Father had wrenched the knife from his hand and lifted him up above his head, for Father is an extremely large and strong man. He marched toward the port side of the ship and threw the man overboard between the ship and the dock.

All eyes stared from Father to the drenched sailor. He pulled himself up onto the pier and marched straightway for the gangplank. He took no more than four steps up the gangplank before Father met him with a cocked pistol.

"You're done with this ship, mate. Come aboard again and I'll be obliged to use this." Father raised the pistol threateningly.

"Ye'll be sorry, cap'n. Tha's all I'll be sayin'."

"Be gone, Smithers. You're not welcome here anymore."

"What about me pay, cap'n. I have coin comin' to me."

"Indeed ye have." Father pulled two ducats from his waistcoat and tossed them on top of the pier. They landed solidly with a metallic sound. Smithers cursed under his breath, but pulled back and scooped up the coins before marching off.

"Any man here wish to challenge my actions?"

Father had turned to face the crew. To a man, they dropped their eyes and returned to their duties.

"I think it's best for you to finish your shopping and return home, Eller."

Aunt Eller nodded and placed a hand upon Father's arm as she passed in front of him. Phillip shook his hand without a word. Father turned to look at me and smiled. "Don't worry about that, my dear. Sometimes the crew gets a little on edge"

"I'm not worried, Father. You're a hell of a man, I've been told. This is the first time I've ever seen it, that's all. I'm quite proud of you, Father. A hell of a man, indeed."

"What?" He laughed. "Now where did my darling little girl learn to talk like that?"

"You did what you had to do."

The others gone down the gangplank, with only Father and I standing by the wheel, I pressed myself into him and kissed him on his cheek.

"Very proud of you. You're a great leader."

"Aye." He blushed at the uncomfortable closeness of our bodies and backed away. "To be captain of a ship and crew, you must lead as fits the moment."

"Kiss me, Father. I shall miss you whilst you are gone."

My father kissed me gently on the cheek and hugged me close to him. He patted me on the bottom as he walked me to the gangplank. I knew from his bravery with the sailor and his firmness as a man in the arms of a woman that if it must be for me to take a husband, I should want a man with the same qualities as my father. I left with a tear in my eye for his leaving and prayed that he would return soon.

Chapter 3
The Count of Selsey

That evening I attended a party with Phillip as my escort. The Count of Selsey was a gracious host with quite an eye for the ladies. The countess, I should note, was not shy when any young squire approached her for a dance.

I stayed close to Phillip, as I knew little of the people in attendance. Most of those who spoke to me spoke of Father and urged that I drop a word in his ear of their fondness and loyalty for him. Phillip confirmed my suspicions by pointing out several of those who had sought me out.

"Pitiful leeches. Nothing to offer but a smile that vanishes the moment your back is turned. Say nothing to your father, for he would have them run through for using you to get to him."

"Father must be more important than I imagined," I said proudly.

"Aye, he supplies most of the storekeepers and his presence on the sea ensures that land holders are not invaded by the Spaniards. The French want mostly to set up their own shops, but the Spaniards will loot the town and ravage all the women."

"And the French would not?"

"The French are more civilized. They prefer to seduce the women." He laughed at the thought. "And so would I for that matter."

"I had better stay close to you, my cousin, lest we be invaded tonight by the Spaniards. You would protect me would you not?"

"If I could persuade you to come to my room, Esther, I would protect you there."

"Ha! As if I would be safe in your room. You have a reputation, I'm told."

A group of wallflowers looked up as we passed by. They had heard my comment and stood there with their mouths open, shocked that a young girl would speak so boldly to a man. Gathering their heads in a huddle, they whispered amongst themselves of how unladylike I appeared, I am sure. When they did not take their eyes off me I whirled around to Phillip, drew him near, and kissed him directly on the lips.

The gasps of air being drawn in by the prudish women could have sucked up the drapery hanging heavily over the windows. Phillip laughed and pulled me close to him. He kissed me deeply and let his left hand stray down to my bustle, which he squeezed.

I moved ahead of him and caught the eye of the count. Approaching me, he let his eyes take in all of my charms and the smile on his face showed his appreciation for the way I was dressed.

"My dear Phillip," he said, his voice a bit too falsetto. "And who is this lovely creature on your arm?"

"Count Armand of Selsey, allow me to present my cousin, Lady Esther Crowley."

"Captain Robert Crowley's daughter?" The count's face lit up as he raised an eyebrow.

"Yes, sir. Captain Robert is my father."

"You are most welcome, my dear." The count leaned low over my breasts, raised my hand to meet his lips and inhaled deeply of the perfume from the cachet I wore within my bosom. "You must honor me with a dance."

I looked at Phillip, who nodded. The count escorted me to the dance floor then across it to a portion heavy with greenery and mostly hidden from the rest of the ballroom. When he drew me to him, I gasped. I had never been held so tightly before.

The count bent his long neck over me and the curls from his powdered wig tickled the sides of my neck. He whispered in my ear a compliment on how divine I looked in my ball gown. In doing so, I felt his hand brush along the outside of my waist and down to the bustle where Phillip had grabbed me moments before.

The count, however, went farther than my cousin. Through his manipulation, the bustle slipped to one side and the count rested his hand on my bum. I did not remove his hand because, to be honest, although he looked like a hound with his long, thin nose and squinty eyes, he was nevertheless familiar with the ladies and I was having a hard time keeping my breath in check.

The count moved against me and attempted to lift my skirt. He pressed his lips to mine before I could resist, then his body jerked suddenly and a grunting sound escaped from his throat. I opened my eyes and saw that Phillip was tapping the count's crotch with a dagger.

"My dear count," Phillip spoke quietly. "I am sure you have other guests more deserving of your attention. My cousin is pure and I intend to see that she stays that way."

"But of course." The count's voice came shakily from lips that had dried noticeably and had drawn tightly across his face. "I do apologize. I became enthralled with her beauty and..."

"We bid you good evening, Count Armand. Thank you for your hospitality."

"Oh, please, don't go. Stay and enjoy yourself. No trouble."

"You are very kind, Count Armand. Some other time, perhaps."

Phillip withdrew his blade and Count Armand breathed a visible sigh of relief. He grabbed his crotch, for assurance I thought, and hurried himself outside as a small wet spot in front of his trousers grew larger and more noticeable.

"Pissy little bastard," Phillip said. "I'm sorry to say, my cousin, but you have developed quite nicely, nice enough and round enough in all the right places that men like that are drawn to. An acceptable lust for any man, but I refer to those like the Count who have no class about them, regardless of their titles."

I looked at my charming cousin half with embarrassment, half with the burning flush at my neck telling me I had enjoyed the touch of the man.

I was truly enjoying this business of being a woman. Overnight it seems I had felt urges I had never experienced before.

"I must say, cousin, that you try my patience severely. As your kin and escort I am sworn to protect you when all the while I feel like taking you away somewhere and doing exactly what that old fop was trying to do to you."

"I...I'm sorry, Phillip. I am going through a strangeness that I cannot explain. experienced the strangest of feelings when he held me; when he tried to..."

"You liked it, didn't you?"

Phillip's hand rested on the side of my waist but held its place.

"Say the word, my teasing little cousin, and I will complete what your wrinkled old lover would have done to you."

"Please, Phillip. Don't be so mean. You are being cruel only because you desire me so much and because you are jealous of any man who looks at me or touches me."

"I have loved you since we were children. How else should I feel about you?"

"Then you should ask Father for my hand when he returns."

"Aye, that I will. Be ye careful, my little seductress; give yourself to no one before your father returns. I shall have you as a virgin lamb so that I and I alone will make you bleed."

"Phillip! That may be how you men talk amongst yourselves, but hold your tongue in front of me. I shall only allow you to go so far in your vulgarity."

"Then kiss me, cousin. Let me feel those wonderfully sweet lips pressed against my own."

The Buccaneer's Daughter

I smiled, because Phillip's voice had changed. He now spoke to me in that bawdy, playful voice to which I was accustomed from him. I had let him kiss me often enough before, but he never took as many liberties as Count Armand had just tried.

I raised myself on tiptoe and offered a kiss to Phillip who, in turn, bent over me and covered my mouth with his. He moved his lips hungrily over mine, parting them with his tongue and probing my mouth deeply. I had to remind myself that we were here at a party where others might see us.

"That's enough, cousin." I stepped away from him and straightened my dress.

"You little teaser," he whispered. "Wait until I give you what you truly want."

Phillip's words held me captive. I was torn between my sense of respectability—not that I had much left, it seems—and the desire he instilled within me by his unabashed need to possess me.

I had always heard that a man should take a woman—any woman, be she harlot or that which he married—and bury himself inside of her with force. It seems to be the man's place to dominate his lover. I'd often wondered why it was expected for a woman to lie back passively and play no part other than willing victim.

I had such strange feelings, such a heat that had overcome me—first with the night thief, then with the count, and now with Phillip. Why should it always be the men who act like wild horses?

Why shouldn't the woman take the reins and ride her stallion until they were both exhausted?

"Save that thought, Phillip. I think it's time for us to leave."

We left the party, and I retired early to my room. All the night I tossed again in the perspiration of desire as I recalled the feeling of the count pressuring me, and wondered what it would be like for Phillip to do the same once we were married.

"Oh, Father, please hurry back so Phillip can ask you for my hand in marriage."

Chapter 4
Lost at Sea

Aunt Eller sat on my bed, crying. She clutched a lace-trimmed handkerchief between her hands and sobbed quietly, looking like she would break loose any moment and gush forth a river from her reddened eyes.

"Aunt Eller? What is it? Why are you crying?"

"Oh, Esther. It's your father."

I jerked upright to a sitting position, the drowsiness of sleep completely gone from my mind.

"What about Father? What's happened to him?"

"Lost at sea, my child. His ship was captured, we're told. His crew enslaved. He and his main crew were killed or thrown overboard."

"Oh, no! When? How?"

"All we know is that *The Neptune* was attacked by a Spanish Man-o-War. The French ship, *Le Cheri*, observed from a distance. Its captain sailed into the waters to look for survivors. They found one, but he died after telling the captain what had happened."

"He saw Father killed?"

"No." She sobbed so hard her hands shook. "He saw the others die, but not your father."

"Then he's still alive."

"No, the French ship found no survivors."

"He must be alive. I won't believe anything else. What news of *The Neptune*?"

"Captured along with part of the crew. It headed toward Portugal, the French did not follow."

I jumped out of bed.

"What are you doing, child."

"I'm going to see the magistrate. Father was patrolling our waters. That means the Spaniards entered our realm. That makes them pirates. I will ask the magistrate to issue a letter of marque for them."

"What good would that do? They have gone."

"I must do something, Aunt Eller. I cannot stay still while there's a chance Father might be alive or that *The Neptune* is still afloat."

"Your cousin, Phillip has already put together a crew. He will look for your father."

"Not without me, he won't."

"No, Esther. You are a child, a female child, you cannot go with him."

"We'll see about that."

I shucked off my nightgown and pulled a set of riding clothes from my closet, donning them as rapidly as I could.

Next, I went to Father's room and armed myself with one of his old cutlasses, a dagger and two of his pistols with lead and powder. I pulled an old hat from deep within his wardrobe and snugged it tight over my hair, which I didn't bother to brush.

I stormed out of the house over the wail of tears and protests coming from Aunt Eller. I never looked back but walked furiously down to the docks, ignoring the stares from the gents and ladies, all the way to where Phillip was standing on the pier in front of a large sloop.

"Are we ready to hoist anchor?" I asked.

"What are you doing here? And why are you dressed like that?"

"It's the most seafaring outfit I could find on such short notice."

"Well, you can just march yourself back home and change clothes. You're not coming with me."

"Yes, I am."

"No, you're not."

"If Father is out there somewhere, I want to be on hand when you find him."

Phillip's voice took a more serious tone. "We may not find him."

"Then I want to be there for that, to pray for his soul."

"You can do that from the church in town."

"I'm going, Phillip, and that's that."

"I said no..."

A loud laugh broke our conversation and the man it belonged to beckoned to us. "Let her come, your lordship. I've no objection."

I looked up to the top of the gangplank. The figure was bathed from behind by the morning sun, which made him a silhouette. Still, I could tell that he was young and hearty looking.

"No, captain, I don't think this is a proper trip for a lady."

The captain laughed again and shook his head in merriment.

"I'm sure she will be safe, m'lord. After all, who would dare trifle with her with both of us protecting her virtue?"

The captain of the ship stepped down the gangplank and I was startled to see it was the young thief who had stolen my necklace. His blond curls cascaded downward over a black tunic trimmed in silver. His plumed hat matched his tunic and his trousers were dark black and tucked inside high-topped brown leather boots. An encased saber slapped his left leg as he moved and I could see half a dozen pistols of various sizes tucked in the silver vest he wore. His mustache and goatee glistened in the morning sun as if freshly waxed. His smile was wide, showing a double row of pure white teeth.

"Welcome aboard, Lady Esther. That is your name, I believe."

"Yes, thank you." I took his hand and walked back up the gangplank looking back at Phillip whose face burned with anger, his hands gripped the map in them so tightly that his knuckles were whiter than the parchment being crushed by his grasp.

"Come along, your lordship," the captain shouted over his shoulder. "Time to weigh anchor."

Chapter 5
Rough Sailing

The first day placed us over halfway to where the French captain had said *The Neptune* had been taken. Phillip and the our thief captain stood on deck and looked over the charts carefully. I joined them and looked over the young captain, very carefully.

He identified himself to us as Captain Trevor Langley, fresh from Jamaica by way of Lisbon and Liverpool.

"I've sailed the Spanish Main and up the Americas over to Newfoundland and back across the Sargasso Sea to London," he said. "I was seeking a much larger ship but I heard of your plight and wanted to join you. I've met Captain Robert before and he did me a kindness. If I am able to repay it, I would be quite happy to do so."

"Was it your plan to steal from my father as way of paying back his kindness," I asked when Phillip took his leave of us. "You know, the night you stole my necklace."

"I'm sorry about that," he said. "I didn't know that was your father's house or that you were his daughter. I was down on my luck and found an open window, which tempted me to see what was inside. I made my way to your bedroom quite by accident, but I'm glad that I did."

He moved closer to me so that our sides touched. I again felt that warmness that was becoming so much a part of me lately. His manliness filled my senses and I had to grip the railing to steady myself.

"This is a fortunate turn of events," he said. "I had hoped to see you again but the Redcoats were quite on edge after that night, and I imagine that included extra security around your townhouse. Still, it would have been worth the risk, seeing you again." His fingers twirled the ringlets of hair falling below my hat. The moisture from the sea air had thickened the strands and left them curly. I shied away from his touch but he stepped closer as he talked. We ended up walking all around the map table as he asked me such personal questions as had I dreamed about him or remembered what he had looked like, or the kiss he had given me.

"Stop, please," I begged him. My head was swimming and not because of the pitch of the schooner. I had my sea legs, but they were becoming more wobbly the closer he came.

"I want you in my bed," he said. "Tonight, when all are asleep save the crew on deck. You must come to me and let me show you how much I can love you."

"As you showed Lady Covington?" I blurted out without thinking. I couldn't help myself.

He stopped moving. His eyes tightened and the muscles in his arms rippled as he closed his fists.

"I hear you had a dandy time with her."

"You seem to be well informed of my nocturnal activities. I'm rather surprised."

"Oh, your nocturnal activities as you say are well known within Portsmouth."

"Then you don't find it strange that I would take a married lady?"

"I may be young, sir, but I am well aware of the physical side of love and the way people carry on."

"Well aware? Of the physical side of love?"

"Sir, I did not intend that to mean I myself have participated."

"Of course, forgive me. It's just that you are so beautiful and I am drawn to you."

"I suspect, sir, that you would be drawn to anyone with breasts and womb."

"I swear, m'lady, I've never heard someone so young speak so plainly about such matters."

"Well, I suppose it is because I was raised by a buccaneer father with no mother to teach me the dainty ways of being a lady. My Aunt Eller has tried, God love her, but she is withdrawn and not forceful."

"And I take it you are rather a handful."

"My father raised me and saw to my education, but he was gone a lot. If I am a handful, as you say, it is not his fault but my own, for I become bored rather easily."

"And you have only recently discovered your romantic side, have you?"

I hesitated.

Should I tell him it was only the night before and that he is the one who awakened my spirit?

Surely that would give him too much information and place me too much under his spell. But, oh, wouldn't that be a welcome place to be. Tonight. His bed. His arms. His lips on mine. I gripped the table harder and my cheeks flushed as I felt a wave of heat start at my toes and work its way up my legs to center in my lower regions.

Our moment together was interrupted by one of the seaman who called to the captain.

"Yes, what is it, McGinty?"

"Better take a look, cap'n."

I stayed rooted near the table while the captain went to the starboard rail and took in the sight pointed out by the first mate. Phillip joined them for a moment then stepped down to the lower deck where I stood.

"What is it?" I asked.

"Sharks," he said. "The captain doesn't seem that concerned about them, but the first mate is."

"Sharks? Would that mean that Father...?"

"We're a whole day away from where your father was put off his ship. Don't jump to conclusions. They're just coming around the schooner looking for Cookie to toss out some garbage. Still, the sea is turning choppy, so you'd best not be too close to the rail if a storm kicks up."

Looking up to the clouds, I could see that they had darkened. A storm was possible. If that were to happen, we could be blown off course. I prayed the sun would come through again and the winds would blow fair and steady to keep us at high speed.

"I'm feeling a bit weak. I think I'll go to my cabin and rest a bit."

"Are you ill?"

"No, I just didn't sleep well last night and I think I'm a bit tired is all."

"Very well. Might as well get some rest. We've a long way to go, anyway."

I left Phillip standing there and stepped below. Turning and closing the door, I saw the captain looking at me and smiling. Once again I felt like the trapped hen with the fox drooling over my flesh. I was vulnerable, I knew. I entered the cabin and laid myself down on the bed. I stared at the wall beside me, imagining I could see a raging fire in the scattered patterns in the wood grain of the panels that covered the walls. I thought about the flames that seemed to be there then remembered the candle atop the dresser to my right. It was unlit because it was still daylight and now that my eyes had adjusted some I could see everything quite well in the cabin. The significance, though, is that I had a candle—an unlighted candle—and no cake. Today was my birthday. I was eighteen.

Chapter 6
A Stranger's Touch

I don't know how long I had slept. It was dark outside and dark inside the cabin since I had still not lighted the candle. Even not being able to see, I was aroused by someone's heavy breathing.

"Who's there?" I whispered.

He didn't speak.

"Please, show yourself."

He did not.

Thinking it was either Phillip or the captain I said, "Come to me then, and let me feel your lips on mine. I will then know which one of you has come to make me fully a woman."

I felt a stirring to my left and a strong hand reached out and touched my breast. I jumped at the touch, but relaxed as the hand cupped my bosom and drew my nipple between the thumb and index finger. I let out a moan and felt a stirring in the pit of my stomach. A warmth came over me slowly; not the rush that I had experienced before, but the soft, warm glow from deep inside that crept over me as my unknown suitor's hand fondled me.

Making himself bolder, I felt his weight upon the bed next to me as he leaned me back and ran his tongue across the tops of my breasts. Warm, rough, like a tabby's tongue, he bathed me with its wetness, tasting my essence even as I heard him inhale my scent. He moved up and over me, lowering himself between my outstretched legs that I couldn't seem to control. As he pressed himself harder against me I was compelled to spread myself wider, eagerly accepting his weight upon my body.

His hands covered my breasts, then dove within the bodice of my nightgown and roughly yanked them free. The coolness of the night caused my nipples to expand, then the warmth of his mouth stilled them as he eagerly sucked each nipple. I was on fire.

He knew fully how to take a woman. He did not rush, but conveyed his eagerness in the way he mouthed my breasts and the constant pressure of his body pressing against me.

His hands gripped the top of my clothing and I heard the cloth tear as he ripped the garment off me.

Next came my riding breeches.

He gripped me from behind. I lifted my hips as he pulled at the waistband and yanked the material down exposing my bum as freely as he had my breasts. He jerked the garment down and I lifted my legs so that he might slip it over my ankles.

I was naked, lying there under him as he pulled back and I heard the rustle of material I imagined was his shirt.

I felt him leave me for a moment and I moaned as if half expecting him to go and leave me so vulnerable. I heard his pants fall to the floor and the heavy sound of his saber hitting the floor.

My pirate captain?

Phillip wore no saber, so it must be Captain Langley. I smiled, although he could not possibly see me doing so in the dark. A tear ran down my cheek. I was awash with emotions I had never felt before. The warmth within my body had built to a fiery volcano and I thought I would erupt at any moment.

I reached for my lover and felt him lower himself upon me once more.

Onions.

I froze.

"Who…who are you?" I cried loudly.

"I'm the lucky bastard wha's gonna take yer maiden's head, ye little whore."

"No! Get off me." I wiggled and squirmed, shrimping my way back toward the headboard of my tiny rack.

"Not on yer life, missy. I've got you now!"

Almost. I knew I was no match for his strength. One more thrust from his hips and my virginity would be gone forever. I reached for whatever ounce of flesh on him I could find and dug my nails in deeply.

"*Owwwww,* shite! Let go of me, ye little bitch."

I held firmly to the side of his ribcage. Clamping my hand tighter, I pulled him toward me. The more I pulled in my direction, the more he pulled away. The stupid buggering fool was hurting himself.

"*Owwwww.*"

The Buccaneer's Daughter

A stream of faint light stabbed its way through the cabin. Light from the stars. I saw the painful expression on the old seaman's face as I squeezed harder. We were a sight, no doubt, naked as we were.

I couldn't tell who it was that had entered the cabin. He swung a boatswain's spike across the top of the old sailor's head and a gush of blood flew out, some of it splattering my arm and face. I saw a stream of crimson, dark in the pale light, run down the man's face. Another blow caused him to close his eyes and he sank back against the wood paneled wall.

I turned to look at my rescuer but all I could see was the outline of his body, dark and unidentifiable, festooned with a luminescent glow circling his body where the dim light shown through the long cotton nightshirt he wore.

He didn't speak. He pushed me back until I was prone on the bed. I tried to see his face, but he was as much a stranger to me as the old lecher had been. I thought at first I was still in danger of being raped.

He made no apology for holding me down on the bed, his rough hand pressing against my bare chest. He leaned over me and I imagined he was looking into my eyes. I could not see his. What would I have seen had there been enough light? A look of lust, perhaps, or a look of disapproval. Maybe sympathy for a poor young girl who had almost suffered an insult at her own folly?

He stood back from my bed. Bending over, he gathered the man's clothes and as he straightened himself he took the man from my bed, hoisting him on top of his shoulders, and turned around to head for the door. He stopped in the doorway with its heavy wooden slats thrown wide. The light of the stars was made brighter by the addition of a half-moon hanging in the blackened sky. My naked body was fully exposed to the man's gaze, and I felt his eyes drinking in every inch of my slim figure.

Then he was gone. The door banged heavily behind him and in less than two breaths from my rapidly heaving chest I heard a faint splash and knew that whomever had come to my rescue had tossed the old fucker overboard. Very well, I thought. Let the sea suck him under and let the fish tear away his flesh as he would have torn away my maiden's head.

I pulled the sheets up around my neck and leaned back against my pillow. I sobbed heavily, my body shaking violently with each rise and fall of my breasts. But I knew it was not just the tears that shook me so harshly; it was the fear of what almost had happened…and my own stupidity. This woman-thing was a dangerous business. I was beginning to see that men could not help themselves. Giving them the idea that I was a willing participant in the game of love—a peach waiting to be plucked and suckled, a whore waiting to be taken—I had placed myself in danger of losing the only gift I could ever give to the man I was going to marry. Oh, what a stupid little girl I still was. I vowed to withhold myself from my non-virtuous desires and offer myself only after someone had placed a ring on my finger.

I stopped crying, but still I shook. My mind was clouded and I did not understand why. The shaking grew more violent and I realized that a part of my mind had remained calm; the part of the brain which gave one what the doctors were starting to refer to as subconscious thought. As I shook deeper and deeper I was aware that my body was revisiting the feeling of the old sailor holding me down. I was responding to the physical, not the mental imagery. Never would I have desired the act of violence without thinking he was one or the other of my lovers, but now that the danger had passed and I recognized my foolishness I rejected the thought of the attack. Too late. The violent shaking grew larger and before I realized what was truly happening I had become that volcano I'd felt before. I was Mount Vesuvius and my bed sheets were the streets of Pompei as I flooded them.

The next thing I knew it was morning, and there was a gentle rapping on my cabin door.

Chapter 7
Searching for Father

Phillip stuck his head in my cabin and smiled. "Are you awake, cousin?"

"Yes."

I didn't know if it was Phillip or the captain that had come to my cabin and saved me from an awful mistake. To be sure I didn't embarrass myself farther, I decided to say little, lest my trembling voice give me away.

"Well, get dressed then. We're nearing the spot where the French said your father was put overboard."

That news shook whatever hesitation from me that I might have had. I jumped from the bed to grab my clothes, forgetting that I was totally naked.

"What's this?" A broad smile crossed Phillip's face.

I jerked my shirt up to cover myself.

"Hah! I wouldn't bother with being modest, girl." He snickered. "You have already shown me a little taste of Heaven and, besides, I've seen you naked plenty of times. But, pray, why are you so *au natural*?"

"Uh, it was a hot night," I lied. Actually, it was a hot night but not in the way I intended Phillip to think. I still didn't know who it was that saved me—saved me from my foolish girlie dreams that had almost got me in trouble.

"It was rather cool, I thought. Maybe tonight I should sleep in your cabin. I could use a hot night with someone as saucy as you."

"Get out of here," I demanded. "I'll join you on deck as soon as I'm dressed."

Phillip laughed and paused a moment while I stood there waiting for him to leave.

I could see he was waiting for me to expose myself again so I did. Getting dressed and looking for Father was much more important than a brief display of skin to a cousin who had indeed seen me naked many times, including a brief moment before.

I threw the shirt over my head and wiggled it down past my breasts while he stood there admiring my form. My dark bush was perky with curls because of the moisture in the air. I slipped my undergarment on before stepping first one leg then the other into my trousers.

"Let's go," I said, and brushed past him to greet the morning.

The sailors were busy cleaning and polishing the fittings, or tending to the sails. The first mate stood in the bow of the ship with a spyglass in his hand as he looked through it over the vast, dark waters ahead of us.

"Do you see anything, McGinty?" Captain Langley yelled.

"Aye, cap'n. Just a bit o' debris, I think. Won't do us harm to check it out. Twelve degrees to port, sir."

"Twelve degrees it is, then." Captain Langley spun the wheel and the mainsail billowed fuller. The schooner pitched to yaw and came about in the new direction. In short order the captain gave the order to take up the sail and to weigh anchor.

"There, cap'n; out there where the debris is the thickest."

The captain stepped from the wheel, letting the boatswain have it. Phillip and I joined him and the first mate at the starboard rail.

"Do you see anything?" I asked. The men clustered in front of me not letting me get too near the rail. "Anything at all?"

"Floaters, missy," McGinty spoke without thinking. Captain Langley gave him a reproachful stare but said nothing.

I knew floaters meant dead bodies so being more frightened at losing Father I pushed my way past Phillip and leaned out over the rail far enough that the captain grabbed me by the waist in case I should fall overboard.

"There!" I shouted. I could clearly see a large man with dark, curly hair and beard clutching to a piece of debris, a portion of the hull of a lifeboat. "Father, oh, Father."

"There, there, Esther," Phillip said pulling me back on deck and out of the captain's hands. "We'll send a grapple out to pull him closer. Keep your worries in check until we are sure."

A sailor had stepped over the railing and braced himself on a porthole window. Another sailor reached over and held him by his wide colored sash.

Swinging the grappling hook above his head, the first seaman let it fly and the triple-hooked grapple landed solidly on the piece of siding near the man's head. One of the points buried itself into the wood and the sailor pulled the rope hand over hand until it was bumping the side of the schooner.

"There!" McGinty yelled. "I see him move, cap'n. He's alive."

"Oh, thank God," I cried and fell back into Phillip's strong grasp.

Two sailors threw ropes over the side where they dangled over the body. The first sailor grabbed them as the second one let his rope go and shinnied down the ropes into the water. He tied one of the ropes around Father under his arms and walked the other rope back up the side of the ship. He and the other sailor grasped the rope holding Father and hoisted him up from the sea, not without difficulty for as I have said before Father was a large man.

"He's alive, sir." McGinty confirmed the fact by raising Father's head and seeing that there was still life in his dark blue eyes.

Badly burned by the sun and worn thin by lack of nourishment, Father nevertheless managed to keep his eyes open until they settled on me.

Blinking severely, as if he might think I was a mirage and his eyes needed focusing, he must have convinced himself that I was real.

He smiled at me and his lips formed the syllables of my name, although no sound came from his vocal chords.

"Father!" I rushed to his side and placed my arm around his neck. His head wobbled as if unattached from his body, but he managed to keep his eyes on me as he tried to speak my name.

"Water," the captain shouted and the cabin boy rushed forward with a dipper in his hands. "Just a little," the captain cautioned and the boy gave Father a sip or two, not allowing him to take the dipper in his own hands.

My father's body stank as if he were a marooned whale dead upon the beach. It was a repugnant smell, but I took in the aroma as if it were a fine French cologne. Each time Father moved an arm or tilted his head, a thrill ran through me. I sat there holding him, never noticing that he had yet to move his legs. It took me a long time to notice that.

In fact, when they stood him to carry him below, he never attempted to stand on his own. It was so strange to see such a big man, a man I had always looked up to, stand there useless of his limbs. The sailors carried him below deck and I fell into Phillip's arms once again and cried deeply.

Captain Langley stood by and watched silently as Phillip comforted me. Just when we were recovering I heard the first mate call to the captain, "Port side, cap'n."

A speck in the distance. A ship. Heading our way?

"Can you see her, McGinty?"

"Nay, cap'n. She's too far away."

"What do we do?" Phillip asked.

"We turn about and pray she hasn't spotted us," the captain said, stepping quickly past us to take the wheel from the boatswain. "We're a smaller ship, harder to see, thank God. She looks to be a Man o' War from the size of her. This isn't exactly a fighting ship."

"But what if she gives chase," Phillip's voice was high with a noticeable concern in it.

"As I've said, your lordship, we're a smaller ship. That's an advantage at this distance. Even so, she has huge sails and can close the gap quickly. But if they haven't seen us we've one more advantage, sir. This is a schooner and she's sleek and meant to run—McGinty, full sail."

"Aye, cap'n."

The first mate didn't have to repeat the command. The sailors on deck had heard the captain's orders and already the main sail was full blown as the captain turned her hard about. The men unfurled the foresail and the schooner leaned leeward with the wind, riding high on the dark inky waters with the waves breaking white, choppy foam against her bow.

"Strike our colors, McGinty. If they make us and give chase close enough to use their spyglass, I don't want them to know that we're English. Let them guess which direction will be our heading."

"But won't they just follow us whichever way we head?" Phillip asked.

"I think they've spotted us, cap'n." McGinty held the spyglass glued to one eye, the other eye squinted shut. "They're getting closer and their sails are full unfurled."

"They'll follow us until they catch us." Phillip's voice faltered as he spoke.

"They can't follow what they can't see, your lordship. Look ahead and see what's in store for us."

In the distance, the clouds had darkened and flashes of lightning jumped about. Below the clouds, a line of rain fell thickly in heavy blue-gray sheets.

"We're in for a blow," McGinty said.

"Aye, mate," the captain smiled wickedly. "And that be our blessing, for see behind us, the ship grows nearer. No doubt now, she's giving chase, all right, but we'll lose her in the storm."

"If we don't lose ourselves first," Phillip complained.

"Which would ye prefer, your lordship: Sure death at the hands of the Spaniards or be in the hands of a loving, forgive ye of yer sins, God Almighty?"

"Go with God, the priests would say," I offered.

Captain Langley looked straight at me, cocked his head, smiled broadly and gave me a wink.

"Then we go with God," he said. "And may God damn the Spaniards all to hell."

I thought about what the captain had said, "...in the hands of a loving, forgive ye of yer sins, God Almighty..."

Would he forgive me of all my sins?

Chapter 8
A Dark and Stormy Sea

The schooner tossed about on the turbulent seas. Waves twice as high as the ship's hull rose above us and crashed down upon our tiny vessel like Thor's mighty hammer smashing fleas, driving us to the deck. We held on to the lanyards, to the rail, to each other. McGinty took me by the arm and guided me to my cabin. He signaled for Phillip to follow.

"I can help topside," Phillip protested.

"Begging yer pardon, yer lordship. I've no doubt ye've got the heart and stomach for it, but fighting a bloody storm like this is no job for a— pardon me, sir—for a landlubber like yourself. There's plenty o' men to handle the ship an' the cap'n is more than a fair hand at the tiller. Leave the ship to us an' either stay in your cabin or give comfort to her ladyship. We'll get through this mess jes' fine. Jes' fine, I say."

Phillip stood his ground, rocky that it seemed because of the pitch of the ship, then nodded his head and stepped into my cabin and shut the door behind us.

For a moment we were in pitch blackness with the door closed and the inky sea rising above the level of the porthole. I found a striker box and scraped the flint across the grooved pipe of steel, lighting the tender and holding it to the wick of the candle until the wick flared and caught. I closed the lid on the striker and placed it back on the table beside the candle.

"It's fine, Phillip." I tried to comfort him. I had never seen him so frightened before. "The storm will play itself out. They always do. Father told me many tales of how he had ridden out the most hellish of winds."

"It's not that, cousin. It's the storm, the pirates, your father alive but in a bad way. I'm afraid I have let everything get to me. Give me my orchards and let me grow my beef, that I can take."

I looped my arm through his and pulled him toward the table in the center of the cabin. He would not take a chair until I had done so. Ever the gentleman, my handsome cousin, always the ladies' man.

As I sat there looking at his face, his brow furrowed and his lips drawn tight over his teeth, the glow from the candle softened the look of his skin and cast tiny scurrying shadows alongside his long, pointed nose and down under the rather large lobes of his ears—the large lobes being a trademark that ran through the generations of men in my family.

The women mercifully had dainty ears for the most part. Father said mine were a copy of my mother's as was my hair, my slender neck and diminutive height. I had inherited most of mother's looks except for my feet and hands. Those I got from my father and they looked large on my small frame, like I was something of a troll. I had to ever look in the mirror to convince myself that the tops of my ears were not pointed and that warts and hair had not sprung about upon my face.

I giggled, and Phillip looked at me questionably. He, no doubt, thought that I had lost my mind with all the wind blowing and the dampness creeping in.

The porous wood sweated from where the water had soaked it. Hardened against all but the most tumultuous splashing of the sea, the schooner was never designed to fight such a vicious ocean.

"It will be over soon," I whispered to Phillip as I patted his hand. Was I trying to convince him or me?

We sat there in silence as I continued to stroke Phillip's hand, then his arm, up to his shoulder and neck. I stood and moved toward him, straddling his legs and settling down firmly on his lap. He leaned back to look at me and rested his hands on my waist.

He stroked the gentle curve leading up to my ribcage until he came to the outside of my breasts. I did not object as he caressed me tenderly. Leaning his face forward, he kissed me.

"Be my wife."

"What?" I wasn't sure I had heard my cousin say those precious three words.

"Marry me, Esther. Be my wife. Have my children. I swear to avoid all other women, to love only you, and to give you the pleasure you so crave. Marry me, cousin, and make me the happiest man alive."

We held each other tightly as the storm outside raged on. Then we fell asleep. When we awoke the crashing sound of waves against the hull were gone.

"What are you thinking?" Phillip asked.

"What it would be like to be your wife," I replied.

The rocking of the ship had eased. Phillip opened the door and stuck his head out.

"Storm's died down," I heard the first mate say.

"Good," Phillip answered him and stepped out on deck.

I followed and marveled at the fresh scent in the air. It seemed that the storm had brought a newness to the ocean, a calmness to the troubled waters.

Captain Langley stared down at me from the steering wheel. When I first caught his eye, he and Phillip had been exchanging words I could not hear. I averted my own eyes.

Looking back, I saw him smiling at me. Innocently or conspiratorially, I did not know. I must have been staring at him longer than I thought. He was a handsome man so perhaps it was natural to stare; but he laughed and winked at me and that brought me out of my reverie.

Phillip had not been smiling but now he, too, flashed a broad smile that lightened up his dark countenance even as the clouds mimicked him and broke to let the sun shine through.

I suppose that is the way with men, that they muddle through dangerous times by instinct then calm themselves afterward through some form of humor.

"No sign of the Spanish ship, cap'n."

"Thank ye, Mister McGinty. Let's keep the sails up and run with the wind."

"Aye, cap'n. That would be my thinking as well."

"Land, ho, cap'n," another sailor said, and Captain Langley strained to look over the bow of the ship.

"Indeed. We are home, my friends."

I was thrilled and joined Phillip and the captain on the upper deck. Standing between them with Phillip's arm around me I looked up at his face.

He was still smiling but he looked at the captain not at me.

I turned to look at Captain Langley and he gave me a warm smile then slipped his arm around my waist over the top of Phillip's.

"I told you there was nothing to worry about, missy. We'll be in harbor soon and I'll personally see to it your father is taken straight away to the doctor."

"As will I," Phillip said and hugged me tighter.

I stood there being held tightly between the two men and felt a slight shudder run through my body. Phillip did not seem to mind that Captain Langley was holding his future wife as tightly as he held me and the feeling that washed over me could only be described as an acceptance that I had two men protecting me. Never had I felt so protected.

After we docked, the captain turned the ship over to his first mate and he, Phillip and I followed two of his sailors who had rigged a gurney and now carried Father down the gangplank onto the dock as we hurried right along to see the doctor.

Chapter 9
Father's Blessing

I sat upon one side of the bed looking at my father as he sipped soup from a spoon being held by a wrinkle-faced midwife who seemed intent on forcing the liquid down him in rapid spoonfuls.

"Give us a break, woman," Father begged.

His voice still weak, his protest was little more than a gesture. Never had I seen him so weak, both physically and in spirit.

"Father, you need to get your strength back." I took the spoon and bowl from the woman and held an offering to his lips, letting him take his time before swallowing it.

"Oh, Esther," Father moaned. "I missed your birthday. I was coming back and intended to be there on time with your present."

I had to fight back a tear or two, but said to him, "Having you here and alive is the only present I need, Father. You have given me a wonderful life, a life of privilege. I would give it all up and live the life of a pauper if it meant having you with me or not."

"My dear child. You are truly a grown young woman."

Weak as he was, Father reached up and stroked my hair and the side of my face. He, too, tried to hold back a tear but a drop trickled down his face anyway.

"All that is important in life is family, someone to love," he said in a weak voice.

I smiled at him and he fashioned a weak smile on his lips.

"I pray you will find someone who will share your life and your love."

Phillip coughed slightly and moved closer to the bed. He placed one hand on my shoulder and inhaled deeply.

"Father, this may not be the right time but I believe Phillip has something he wishes to say to you."

The room grew dark as clouds gathered outside obscuring the morning sunshine. Father looked at Phillip waiting to hear what he had to say.

"Indeed," Phillip said, stepping forward. "You see, sir...ah, what I mean to say is...as to your daughter and I...I mean, if you would agree..."

"Esther!" Father's voice rose louder than before. "Could you at least have found someone to marry who can intelligently finish a sentence?"

"Uncle Robert, may I please have the honor of having your daughter's hand in marriage, if you please, sir?" Phillip's nervous request tumbled out in a rapid falsetto.

"That's more like it." Father dropped his head back on the pillow. "And do you love my daughter and intend to keep her in the manner in which she is accustomed?"

"Yes, sir."

"Good. I want lots of grandchildren. You'd best get after it, boy."

I shrieked. Phillip turned red as a beat and the others in the room laughed heartily.

"Esther," Father spoke more seriously, "I can't move my legs. The doctor thinks I have spinal damage. I won't be able to run the business as well as before."

"Don't worry, Father. We'll do fine. Phillip is a good businessman, and…"

"Phillip, you are a good horticulturist. Your orchards are plentiful. You know the earth and what it takes to produce from it. But I am a man of the sea, a buccaneer, and that is another business altogether. I need a man to sail my ships. *The Neptune* may be gone but I can buy other ships. What I need is a man who can trim the tiller with one hand and wield a cutlass with the other."

Father turned his head slightly to the left of us.

"Captain Langley, you saved my life and for that I am grateful. Will you sail for me?"

"Aye, sir." Captain Langley stepped up behind me and placed both his hands on my shoulders. "I'll take care of everything that's yours as if it were my own."

Captain Langley's hands upon my shoulders did not escape Father's scrutiny, yet he said nothing.

I could see in his eyes that he was concerned, but I couldn't understand why. To me, the captain was only being a friend.

Father looked from me to Phillip and back to Captain Langley again.

"Your first mission will be a dangerous one," Father told the captain.

"I've never been one to run away from a good fight, sir."

"Good, because it's a fight you'll have. I want you to go after that bastard Diego and get my ship back."

"It was Diego?" I moaned.

"Yes, that's the second time that slippery Spaniard has taken something from me. This time he had help."

"Help?" Captain Langley asked.

"Aye, that no-good snake, Smithers. After I kicked him off *The Neptune*, he signed with that black hearted Diego and told him where to find me on the high seas. You catch Smithers, hang him for me."

"It'll be my pleasure, sir."

"I need my rest," Father said. All of the talking had made him weak again and so we bade him close his eyes and sleep. We left him there to rest while we made other plans.

"I shall inform the crew," Captain Langley said. "I believe all of them will stay. When your father is stronger, we will discuss what ship to buy."

"Meanwhile," I said. "I will find Aunt Eller and make plans for the wedding."

Phillip smiled and kissed me. "I shall leave the details up to you, my sweet. I have some people who must be added to the list. I will give those names to mother and you can address the invitations."

"Am I invited?" the captain asked.

"Of course," I said. "You are already close enough to be family, having saved Father's life. I wouldn't think of not inviting you."

"Good, that means I get to kiss the bride." He grabbed me and pulled me to him, giving me a peck

on the cheek. He looked at Phillip and smiled a wicked smile. "You don't mind do ye, yer lordship?"

"No," Phillip said, his voice dropping in tone. "I don't mind. It seems that Esther likes you well enough, so it looks like the three of us will be quite close."

"Ah, you like me, Lady Esther?"

The strangest feeling came over me, washed over me like the roaring waves that had almost carried us to our death. "Yes, I do like you. If my future husband does not mind."

What was I saying? Was I implying anything I should not? I don't know where the words came from. I just blurted them out without thinking. I know being raised by a rough-edged buccaneer had robbed me of any real ladylike training and speaking my mind was as common to me as it was to my father. I was truly my father's daughter. Now, it seems I was about to be married to one man, yet attracted to another.

I had not expected this kind of development but here I was in the arms of one while the other looked on. I was thankful the good doctor had no other patients coming and going, for we were bare upon the street for any passersby to look at us and wonder what kind of woman carried on so with two men so familiar with her.

"I'll take another kiss after the wedding," the captain said.

"We need to go," Phillip said. He reached forward and grabbed me, pulling me away from the captain.

"Ye're a lucky man, my friend. I look forward to being in business with the both of ye."

My body shimmered in pleasure at the sound of his words. Phillip undoubtedly felt the tremor in my body and mistook it for a response to his own touch.

"Oh, Esther, I am sure we will be a most happy couple."

"We'd better hurry," I said. "I'm still very tired and shall fall down to sleep in the street if I don't get home and get into bed."

Chapter 10
Wedding Bells

After waking the next morning, Aunt Eller and I spent all that day planning a wedding list, ordering the cake, and arranging for a seamstress to come for my measurements and a first fitting.

Standing still for the fitting was a tedious task, for I had so many things on my mind. Phillip had presented me with a gorgeous diamond and pearl ring and I could not stop looking at it. I held my hand at arm's length and saw how the sunlight coming through the glass of the French patio doors bounced off the stone in corrugated plumes filling the eye with the colors of the rainbow as I twisted my hand in first one direction then the other.

"Stand still," Aunt Eller scolded me. "How is she to ever get the seam straight with you bouncing around so?"

"Oh, Auntie, isn't it beautiful?" I asked, holding my hand up for her to see.

"Yes, yes, of course. The ring is beautiful, you are beautiful and if you hold still for a moment, your wedding dress will be beautiful."

"Oh, I don't care. I shan't be wearing it that long, anyway."

"Esther!" Aunt Eller squealed, then choked back her laughter.

The seamstress, Miz Hattie Brown, raised her hand to her mouth to stifle a giggle. Her face flushed, but she calmed herself and went back to pinning the bottom of the dress to keep the hem level.

"Well, isn't that what happens after the bride and groom are alone?"

"Yes, my dear, but we normally don't talk about it."

"Well I want to. Phillip is a powerful man, rich I mean, a good businessman. He is handsome, charming, and he loves me. He will be a good lover, I am sure."

"Esther?"

I blushed and silently berated myself for my boldness. Aunt Eller was right, young ladies do not talk that way, even amongst themselves. But that was my father's way of talking and, after all, I was a buccaneer's daughter, was I not?

The day ended with a perfectly fitting dress and replies coming in from family and friends, most of them saying they would attend. All things in place for the end of the week.

Finally free of responsibilities for the day, I looked in on Father.

"How are you doing?" I asked.

"Stronger," he replied. "But I still have no feeling from the middle of my back down to my toes. The doctor fears that I have severed my spine. But at least I'm alive thanks to you and Phillip and that young captain."

"Do you truly trust him to take over your ships?"

The Buccaneer's Daughter

"One ship. I had most of my money tied up in *The Neptune* and in the house and other lands I had bought. I have enough to purchase a galleon and let him hire a crew. He will have to pull in a good bit of bounty in his first forays at sea if he intends to keep a full crew on board."

"Father, all of the jewelry you have given me over the years…is it worth much?"

He thought about that for a moment. A puzzled look crept across his face and he answered slowly, watching his words carefully.

"Aye, some of it. Some are just pretty baubles, but there's a piece or two in there that the Queen herself would be proud to wear. Why do you ask?"

"Take it. Take it all. Sell it and use the money for what you need."

I rarely wore but a few rings and a few pearls when we had a dance, so I would not miss the bulk of it. I could keep a few pieces Father had given me as special gifts and let the rest go.

"There's more than enough in there to finance at least the food for the galley and maybe some powder and shot," I told him.

"Yes, there's more than enough for those items. But I can't take your jewelry; I won't take it. A woman must go to her new husband with a full dowry. Leave the business to me, daughter, and be happy for finding a husband."

"I am, Father—happy enough, that is."

"Remember that it is common practice to keep the royal blood free by marrying within the family tree."

"Oh, Father, you made a rhyme."

"Ha! Indeed I did."

"I'm not concerned with what others might think. After all, the king married…what is she, a third or fourth cousin of mine?"

"She is the queen. Leave it at that."

"I do wish you and King George would try to be friends again. You were so close growing up."

"We were as children. But men form their own minds and their own principles and prejudices as they get older. George has his ways and I have mine."

"And you got the girl before he did." I couldn't help myself, I giggled.

"Oh, ha-ha-ha. Please, Esther, don't make me laugh so, it hurts."

"I was just trying to make you feel better. Tell me, Father, is it true that you were quite the ladies' man before you and mother were wed?"

"Now you're embarrassing me, Esther. That kind of talk is rhetoric for the pub, something to be shared with other men. Something that men brag about amongst themselves."

"And does Phillip ever brag of his conquests?"

"Your future husband is a man of dignity and quiet strength. He doesn't have to brag, because we know that he is indeed man enough to take a woman and make her feel wonderful."

"Yes," I said with a sly smile on my face, "I'm sure he is. I'm sure that I am quite the lucky one to have had him propose."

"Sometimes going through a bit of danger, like that storm, brings a young couple closer together. I can see that that is the case. Esther, I would not ask just how close the two of you became that night, but I will say that I am quite happy for both of you."

"Father, you are truly a wise man."

"Then you have no doubts then about getting married to him?"

"None, whatsoever."

"I am pleased."

I kissed my father on the cheek and left so that he could continue to rest. I, too, needed to rest. It wasn't that I was tired, it was nerves. I needed to calm myself. Thinking of Phillip and our night together at sea, nearly losing our lives; and what our wedding night would be like did nothing to settle my nerves. I couldn't sleep.

I had to force the thoughts out of my mind. Counting sheep did no good, so I decided to take a walk in the garden. Night had settled in and the stars were shining. I listened to the crickets chirping their songs of love and heard the occasional grunt of a bullfrog.

The sounds of nature had always soothed me. Tonight I was grateful for a clear night with no fog, no rain. Less than an hour passed and I was ready to return to my room.

The next day passed, and the next, and Saturday came. Fresh flowers greeted me as I entered the formal area and their fragrance continued as I stepped out into the garden. Tables and chairs had been placed under tents, and Aunt Eller was busy giving instructions to two young boys setting up the arbor under which Phillip and I would exchange vows.

The guests arrived on time, as did the food and the local minister. I heard a few muttered voices complaining about not holding the wedding in a church, and a few more voices who defended the idea with snide remarks that as a buccaneer family, the church was afraid it would be short a candlestick or two if we had the wedding there. Let them talk. You can't change the way people think, and today the only people who mattered were the bride and groom.

"I can't walk you down the aisle." Father sounded so downhearted.

"I'll be happy to push your wheelchair, sir," Captain Langley said. The captain wore a French silk jacket with gold roping and large buttons. Lace spilled out at his throat and his doeskin pants fitted so snugly I heard many of the women giggle when he passed them by. His boots were shiny black with gold tips on the toes and a leather-fringed tassel at the top edge, dangled along the side that swayed when he walked.

"Thank you, captain, it seems I need your services on land as well as sea."

"My services are always available." He said to Father, but he looked straight into my eyes when he said it. Father didn't notice, for his head was bowed forward looking at his imprisoned legs. Someone had strapped them to the chair so they would not slip and dangle. Otherwise, he looked splendid in a patterned purple coat and his best green hat which bore a plumed Ostrich feather.

The music began to play which signaled everyone to take their seats. The three of us remained behind a large tree waiting for the bridal march. I could see Phillip through the branches of the tree and he stood tall and proud in his Home Guard uniform. He held the rank of brigadier. I was so proud of him. His hands, though. I noticed his hands could not keep still. Holding them behind his back, he could not stop them from fidgeting. The groom is always nervous, they say, more so than the bride. That's probably not true. I was so nervous I wanted to pee. We took our places and the minister began to speak.

"We are gathered here today in holy matrimony. If anyone can show just cause as to why this couple should not be joined together, let him speak now or forever hold his peace."

That's as much as I remember until we got to the part where we both said, "I do."

"You may now kiss the bride."

There it was. I was Lady Esther Crowley of Mountbatten...Mrs. Phillip Mountbatten. We took our wedding walk through a hail of flowers being thrown by the guests and an archway of sabers from Phillip's regiment. We stopped at the reception tent, where we cut the cake with a saber.

The guests were still milling about, chatting feverishly, when I bid goodbye to Father. He patted me on the shoulder and on the tops of my hands.

"My little girl," he said, almost crying. "All grown up."

"I shall always be your little girl, Father."

It was over. As happy as I was to be a new bride, I was also exhausted. I knew there was a long night ahead of me and in truth, I looked forward to it with only a small degree of enthusiasm. All I really wanted to do was let Phillip carry me over the threshold and put me to bed...so I could sleep.

But I would give myself to my husband because that is what married women do. He loves me and I love him and tonight would be special.

I whispered in Phillip's ear that I was ready and he agreed. Phillip, however, had celebrated a little too heavily and could not find his footing very well. He stood, weaved, almost fell into Captain Langley who caught him and propped him upright.

Phillip had a sideways grin on his face that looked comical. We all laughed at him.

"Maybe I'd best give ye a hand getting him into the carriage," the captain said.

"Maybe you'd better," Phillip agreed.

"Yes, maybe you'd better," I said.

We managed to get Phillip settled inside the closed in hansom with the captain across the seat from him, leaving a spot for me next to my overly inebriated husband. The captain signaled to Phillip's driver who took his place and turned the horses about. Inside the carriage, dark as pitch, I could hear Phillip begin to snore.

"We should be arriving soon," Captain Langley said.

And soon we did. The captain helped me pull Phillip from the carriage who was now awake enough to stumble his way to the front door.

"I must carry you over the threshold, Esther."

"I don't think you're in any shape to do that, Phillip."

"Oh, yes, it is my duty as your husband."

Phillip unlocked the door, kicked it open with his boot and lifted me in his arms. He stumbled a little and I thought he would drop me, but with the captain's help he straightened up and hoisted me higher. His arms felt strong and he moved easily. Captain Langley followed until Phillip got me just inside the doorway.

"I think I can handle things from here," Phillip said to the captain.

Captain Langley's face registered surprise and he looked from Phillip to me and back to Phillip. I expected him to say more, but he didn't.

"Of course, your lordship. I bid ye goodnight."

The captain bowed to us both and backed away to appropriate a ride back to Father's house, I presume. Phillip kicked the door closed and prepared to mount the stairs with me in his arms."

"Phillip, you'll drop me."

"Nonsense my dear. I'm as sober as a Catholic priest and I'm not tired at all. We have a long night ahead of us."

I didn't know what to expect. If Phillip had been sodden as he had seemed, what a miracle that he could recover so quickly.

Had he been as drunk as he had seemed? I couldn't tell.

Phillip managed to get me up the stairs and into our bedroom without dropping me. He placed me upright and turned me toward him. He looked at my partially unbuttoned blouse and smiled.

"You had some fun coming home to your new house."

"Phillip…I…no, it must have come undone when you lifted me."

We moved to the wedding bed and Phillip finished stripping my wedding gown from me. He dropped his clothing, as well. We wrapped ourselves in each other's arms and made slow, passionate love.

I don't remember falling asleep. Sometime during the night I woke up in Phillip's arms. His breathing was strong but slow and even, keeping a rhythm that remained steady and quiet. I had always heard that men snored. I closed my eyes and snuggled against my husband's chest glad that he didn't. I felt the drowsiness creep over me again and I was almost asleep when I heard Phillip inhale deeply…and start to snore.

Chapter 11
The Carriage Ride

The sun broke through the window as I opened my eyes.

Phillip was already up. He had left a note on his pillow. No words, just a drawing of a heart with his initials underneath. I smiled and tucked it under my pillow. A knock sounded on my door. The door opened even before I could answer and a woman only slightly older than me waltzed in carrying a breakfast tray.

"G'morning, mum. The mister, he said to fetch ye some breakfast. I dinny know what ye might like, so I haves ye some o' this and some o' that."

She sat the tray down upon my lap and unfolded a napkin, planning on tucking it in at the top of my nightgown. She stopped when she realized that I wasn't wearing a nightgown or anything else except the bed sheet.

"Oh," she startled, "beggin' your pardon, mum. I'll jes' leave ye to yer breakfast and come back in a little while to fetch the tray."

"What is your name?"

"Oh, silly me, I forgot yer've never been here before. Me name is Alice Minever, mum. I be the maid and housekeeper and sometimes the cook if me sister gets one o' her headaches."

"Does she often get headaches?"

"Only on the morning after she's had a bit too much to drink, mum." Alice made a motion with her hand to show the tipping of a bottle, then laughed.

"I take it that your sister likes to make the rounds of the taverns."

"Aye, she's a popular lady with the men, mostly seamen, you know. I don't care much for their lot, but me sister is a bit on the chunky side, you know, an' she don't get no regular callers. But I must say, she seems to have an awful lot o' fun in her own way."

"I think that's smashing. And what do you do for fun?"

Alice suddenly stiffened and brushed off her apron as if she had spilled something on it.

"I'd best be getting to the rest of me duties, mum. Enjoy yer breakfast, mum."

She left the room and left me wondering. She had plenty of talk about her sister, but nothing to say for herself. She was too young and too pretty to be an old maid, so I had to figure either she'd had a bad experience with a lover or was too shy to even have one...or perhaps she was involved with a married man and didn't wish to explain that. Whatever her reasons, I was sure we would get along. She was easy enough to talk to about other things. My curiosity did not demand to be satisfied right away, for the smell of the bacon and eggs was tantalizing and after last night's round of lovemaking, I was famished and needed to regain my energy.

The Buccaneer's Daughter

I ate slowly, savoring each bite. The eggs were fresh, the rasher of bacon was cooked crisp and the blackened bread and jam complimented the meal. I sipped the hot tea with honey and saved the fresh squeezed orange juice for last so I would have a sweet taste in my mouth.

Another knock on the door announced Alice's return. She said nothing, but gathered the tray with a polite smile and curtsey. I had no idea how to dress for the day. I chose riding clothes because I expected to find Phillip in his orchards overseeing the workers. I opened the armoire and selected jodhpurs, a blouse, a jacket and riding boots. I did not want headgear because I wanted the wind in my tresses. As the old saying goes, I wanted to feel free as the breeze.

I bolted down the staircase and was about to step outside when the door opened and Captain Langley stepped inside.

"Ah, there you are, and already dressed, I see."

"And what did you expect to find, me running around without a stitch on my body?"

"That would have been a beautiful sight, I am sure."

We both laughed at that. Alice walked past with the bed sheets in her arms, no doubt prepared to wash them. She flashed a disapproving look in our direction but being the good servant, said nothing.

"Phillip said you were sleeping when he left. He said I should wake you and carry you with me to look at the ships. He will be in the fields all day and thought a day alone would be boring for you."

"But I was just on my way to find him."

"No, you were just on your way to help pick out your father's new ship."

Those dark eyes were sparkling mischievously at me, and his bow was low enough and graceful enough to be addressing the queen. The man was a charmer. I had not forgot Aunt Eller's warning about him, nor had I forgot how familiar he was with me even in front of Phillip. There was so much magnetism about him that I felt weak in the knees whenever he smiled at me like he was doing now.

"All right, let's go pick out a ship." I smiled and took the arm he offered.

He had an enclosed coach waiting, which was a good thing because the clouds were dark and threatening. The captain helped me inside the compartment and closed the door. The driver snapped his whip and the team began a slow walk past the low hedges that accentuated both sides of the cobblestone driveway. Apparently the driver already knew the destination for the captain said nothing to him and concentrated all his attention on me.

We had not gotten past the end of the driveway and onto the long road leading to the main highway before the driver drew the team of horses to a halt and Captain Langley opened the carriage door for us to dismount.

Chapter 12
The Tall Ships

The driver helped me out of the carriage and Captain Langley took me by my arm to escort me along the pier to observe the ships docked in the bay. The captain pointed to a tall mast ahead of us. As we walked past the scores of goods piled high upon the deck I could see the length of the ship and count the canon hatches, six of them, which meant there were also six on the port side. The name under the ballock said *Enchanted Princess*, and the teakwood windows were smooth and shiny with carved dolphins coming up each side as if they were rising out of the sea. Dolphins are a sign of good luck to sailors, Father told me, because they are considered a sign that land was nearby.

The canvass sails on the ship we inspected were tied properly and the fittings were polished. On her bow, the carved effigy of a young woman pointed a finger forward on her left hand. Her arm, extended as it were, was lithe and graceful. The garment covering her was made to slip past her right shoulder and down over her breasts with the left one covered and the right one exposed. Her right hand cupped her breast, leaving the nipple large and unobstructed. Superstitions among the sailors suggest that the extended hand gives guidance while the cupped breast promised sustenance for the journey.

The captain paused at the gangplank but nobody gave him concern.

"Ahoy, the ship," he called out and a bearded sailor peered over the railing to look at us.

"Permission to come aboard," the captain called out again.

"Permission granted," the sailor replied. "Who be ye, matey?"

"Captain Langley in search of a ship."

"Aye? Then hurry ye steps, cap'n; time's a-wastin' and she's a good one for the taking."

"Is the master on board?"

"Nay, jes' us sailors. But ye can 'ave a look roun' if ye like. Ye'll find the master down the planks at the sail cutters. We had a problem with one o' our jibs last time at sea an' the master wants to replace the sail."

"An' what about yer cap'n? Is he with the ship's master?"

"Nay, the cap'n got hisself kilt in a row with an English scoundrel. Maybe ye knows 'im; goes by the name Smithers."

"Aye, I've heard of him. Sailing with the pirate Diego, I hear."

"Ye hear right, cap'n. Those two bin tearin' up the sea roun' the nor' point. Say, are ye lookin' to sign on or purchase 'er?"

"Purchase, if the price is right."

"Well, ye'll 'ave to talk to the master 'bout that. He's a mind to let 'er go, I can tells ye that much; but yer biddin' is yer own business, sir."

"Thank ye for the information, matey. I'll be happy to do some talking to the owner."

"An' who de ye bring with ye on such a bright mornin', if I may be so bold as to ask. She's the spittin' image o' our carved princess."

"This is Lady Esther Crowley of Mountbatten...Mrs. Phillip Mountbatten. It's her father who's buying the ship. I'm just acting as his agent."

"Lady Esther Crowley? Cor, and sure you not the daughter of Cap'n Robert Crowley?" The sailor stepped back a step and doffed his straw hat. He bowed deeply to show his respect of my father and to me as his daughter. "Ah've sailed under Cap'n Robert a time or two, missy...er, Miz Mountbatten. He's as fine a gentleman as ever turned a wheel, and a great leader of men."

"Thank you, Mister...?"

"Oh, beggin' yer pardon, ma'am. Me name is Conner...Conner O'Riley. I'd like to say it's a pure pleasure to have ye on board."

"We're off to find the master and strike a bargain," Captain Langley said.

"Aye, cap'n. We'll be here when ye return. I s'pose ye'd like to take 'er roun' the bay a bit if'n ye close the deal."

"Aye, that would be my desire. Have her ready for me, Mister O'Riley. I can almost guarantee that she'll be sold within the hour."

"Aye, cap'n." The sailor turned to shout over his shoulder. "Awright, lads; ye heared the cap'n. Look lively, now. Loosen the lanyards and be ready to weigh anchor within short order."

"Aye-aye, Cap'n O'Riley," the others mocked the man. O'Riley took the humor well enough and even blushed a little under the dark tan of his cheeks. "She'll be right ready when ye return." He winked at us.

Captain Langley and I exited the ship and strolled down the boardwalk looking for the sail shop. We found it soon enough and the master of the ship was delighted that we made him an offer. He turned it down, of course, as we knew he would. That is part of the deal, dickering for a mutually satisfying price. The captain countered his demands and they went back and forth one more time each before they shook each other's hands. Only then did Captain Langley tell the man that it was being purchased by Captain Robert, the most famous sailor in Portsmouth. Had he known it was Father, he would have had more respect in his voice and more respect for Father's gold, meaning he would have asked a higher price.

Captain Langley handed the man a note of script for the bank and the man scribbled a hasty bill of sale. He would leave a more formal one at the bank, as was the custom under English law, for the bank would hold it in Father's name along with all the other property notes Father kept there.

We returned to the ship and Mister O'Riley piped us aboard and saluted his new captain. Soon we made our way out of port and the sailors unfurled the sails to their fullest. She was a grand ship, leaning westward against the wind, but jutting this way and that around smaller vessels until she had the open sea to herself and Captain

Langley himself turned her with the wind and let her fly.

When he had satisfied himself that she could sail true to course, he turned the ship's wheel over to O'Riley and told him that I was feeling tired and wanted to rest. The captain did not wait for a reply, but took me by the arm and gently pointed me towards the captain's quarters. Captain Langley left me therein and returned to the wheel to have fun with his new beauty. He came for me an hour later after I had napped a bit.

Chapter 13
The Isle of Wight

We stepped out of the cabin to stroll on deck and see how the *Enchanted Princess* handled the heavy waves. The Isle of Wight loomed ahead of us and Captain Langley gave orders to take the southern route instead of the inlet between it and the mainland.

Lovers' Island, some called it. There were stories aplenty about pirate ships mooring themselves offshore whilst the officers and some of the men went ashore with women prisoners they had captured from the Spanish or French ships; mostly French women as the stories went, but I think that was because the French are supposed to be so bawdy and that thought added spice to the stories. Anyway, many a young woman was supposed to have lost her virginity on the southern coast of the island.

"Mister O'Riley, prepare the longboat," Captain Langley commanded.

"Aye-aye, cap'n." O'Riley didn't repeat the order to the crew. I suppose he didn't want to be made fun of again in front of the new ship's captain. The other sailors, though, knew what to do and lowered the longboat over the side. Someone tossed a net over the side of the ship, and that made it easier for me to climb down amongst the men. A few of them snickered seeing the material of my jodhpurs stretched tight over my buttocks, but they quieted themselves immediately. I'm sure the captain's gaze was not that friendly, so they went about their tasks waiting until I had my feet planted solidly upon the boat's decking.

The men rowed as the captain stood forward leaning against the covered bow. I sat quietly and watched him with much pride knowing that such a man as he, such a powerful leader of men, was personally chosen by my father and impressed me with such passion for the open sea.

How quickly I had forgotten the first time we had laid eyes on each other, how quickly he had turned my resolve to mush, how easily I had fallen for his smile. Oh, he was a charmer, this one, but such as Aunt Eller had warned me about. Still, I couldn't help but smile each time he smiled at me.

"It's beautiful," I said as we got closer to the beach.

The sand was nearly a pure white and littered with bits of pink coral and brown seashells at the water's edge. Small crabs danced sideways as they hastened to wherever it was they were going. The blue sky was a gigantic canvas overhead painted with high, billowy white clouds.

The image was broken by a handful of sea gulls that floated over us from ship to shore, gliding effortlessly on currents of air. Their high-pitched calls bade us welcome to the island. We landed in a wash of dark-green seaweed, carried ashore by the white-capped waves and foamy flow of the tide.

Captain Langley jumped from the boat and nodded to O'Riley who scooped me up and handed me over the edge and into the captain's waiting arms.

"No sense in yer feet getting wet, m'lady." Captain Langley smiled. He carried me to dry sand and stood me upright with only a casual closeness of our bodies. I had the strangest urge to not let go of his grip around my waist.

I calmed myself and, instead, turned to head inland. Ahead of us were huge rocks and a row of palm trees. Gray colored driftwood lie scattered about and some of the men gathered up double armloads and began laying it out in front of the rocks for a campfire.

"Should we go any farther?" I asked, "Since we don't have rifles or pistols, could it not be dangerous?"

"Nobody lives here, love," the captain said. It was the first time he'd called me that. I didn't know if he was being flirtatious or just caught up in the romantic surrounding of the island. It did, I recalled, have that erotic history if you believed in the stories about this place. "And if it's animals we run into, we have our cutlasses and I do have a pistol."

"Oh, well, if you think it's safe enough."

"Besides, there's something I want to see, over here I think."

He led the way while O'Riley and I followed. Captain Langley hacked through some vines with his cutlass and spread them back from a huge rock with strange writing on it.

"What does it say?" I asked.

"How the bloody hell do I know?"

His tart answer stopped me cold. It was vicious, and even caused O'Riley to pause in his tracks.

"This is what I expected," the captain said.

He opened the heart-shaped locket he had stolen from me the first night we met and placed it alongside the hieroglyphics painted on the rock.

"Here, see? You place the locket under the pictographs and match it to the two hearts drawn side by side, see?"

I didn't see. I mean I saw the two hearts painted on the rock and I saw the locket in the captain's hand, but I didn't see what he wanted me to see, but apparently the first mate understood right away.

"The arrow in the locket, sir?"

"Quite right, Mister O'Riley. The arrow points in the direction where the treasure is buried."

"Treasure? What treasure? I'm confused," I said.

"Buried treasure, my dear. The stories I've heard tell about it, why a man could be rich enough to own the island, to own all of Portsmouth even."

"Jes' a tale, I'm told," O'Riley said.

"Ye've seen the sign, O'Riley. Do I have yer loyalty or do I have yer heart on the end of me cutlass?" He lifted his cutlass and was now pressing it against O'Riley's chest.

"I sail wi' the mast, cap'n. I do what ye asks o'me."

"Ye're a smart man, O'Riley. Jes' don't get too smart. I'll share whatever we find here."

"I'm happy to hear that, cap'n."

"Back to the beach and not a word of this from either of ye."

"Aye, cap'n."

"But Trevor...I mean, captain...what about...?" It was the first time I'd addressed him by his first name.

"Not a word, my love, if ye don't want one of them scoundrels slipping up on you tonight and slicing that pretty little throat of yours. Gold makes men do evil things."

"They would kill us for the gold?"

"In a bloody heartbeat, they would. At least, Mister O'Riley and me would be done in quickly. You, they would keep around until all of the rum was gone and every one of them had jollied himself with you three or four times."

I drew in a quick breath and O'Riley stifled a laugh. I didn't understand why the captain would speak so vulgar. Was it lust for the gold or his way to say he truly fancied me?

We arrived back at the campfire just as the first stars were twinkling in the orange and purple sky above us. Some of the sailors had caught crabs and others had set up a pot of water over the fire to boil the catch.

What a night this might be. I hadn't been camping since Phillip and I had spent the night out on the grassy plains behind Father's house when I was just twelve years old. Phillip, although older than me, had not tried to do anything to me then, but I had caught him pleasuring himself that night without him knowing I was watching. Now that we were newlyweds I wished he were here with me tonight so we could cuddle beneath the stars and eat crabs together and...oh, my...my imagination was running away with me.

Chapter 14
Back to Port

The night was simply boring. No jokes, no ghost stories, and nobody paid that much attention to me, not even the captain.

He sat off to one side talking quietly to O'Riley. Whatever was on their minds didn't include me.

A few of the other men cast fleeting glances in my direction but I guess they figured I was really the captain's woman--or worse, Captain Robert's daughter and they didn't want the problems that could come from messing with a buccaneer princess.

Of course, they hadn't heard about Father being paralyzed, but even then they probably wouldn't have been brave enough to risk his wrath by messing with me. So I slept until morning in a makeshift hammock one of the sailors had rigged for me. He was cute in a tanned and skinny way, and I thanked him.

When I awoke, a bright blue sky hovered above me, with almost no clouds in sight. The seagulls were up and about and one even landed on the end of my hammock until I moved then it flew away. I arose and looked for a private spot to do my morning business. I started off toward the tree line and a cluster of large rock.

"Beggin' yer pardon, ma'am," one of the black sailors approached me. "I bests go wid ye, part ways that is, jes' in case there be wild animals up an' about. It's their time, ye see. I promises I won't get too close while ye ducks behind a bush."

"Thank you. I see that you're a real gentleman."

"Me? Ha! Don't be so trustin' o' the likes ye see here. We's all men and ain' nuttin' gentle 'bout none o' us. I tells ye plain."

"Well, I ain't no high-born lady myself." I shook my head back and forth.

"Oh, but ye're more lady than any o' these men eber see, thot's for sure."

"Well, I thank you for your courtesy," I said and headed for the tree line again with the black falling in behind me.

True to his word, he stopped short as I reached the line of trees and even turned his back so he faced the ocean. He crossed his arms and stood on guard with his cutlass dangling from a sash around his waist.

I couldn't help from comparing him to a palace guard at Cleopatra's court. When I had finished my business, he walked me back to the longboat where the captain and O'Riley had gathered the men. Fresh coconuts in their arms, the crew boarded and took up their long oars to row us back to the *Enchanted Princess*.

Back on board ship, Captain Langley gave the order to withdraw the anchor and unfurl the sails. In a short time, we were under sail again heading back to Portsmouth.

Captain Langley hardly spoke a word to me the entire return. I wasn't sure if he was simply busy or had I displeased him in some way.

We were soon docked again in Portsmouth and he hailed a cab, bid goodbye to the crew, and we went clippity-clop back to Father's townhouse for him to present the temporary bill of sale to Father and tell him all about the frigate.

"She's a fine ship, sir. Ye'll like her, I'm sure."

"I shan't be going with you," Father said.

"Not going?"

"My legs won't do me well. I'm afraid my sailing days are done. You will have to hunt down Diego and do my killing for me."

"Aye, that I can do. But it's yer ship, sir, and ye should see her for yourself. If it's yer reputation ye're concerned with," he leaned closer and whispered, "We can wrap ye up and carry ye on board, telling the crew that ye're a bit under the weather and won't be sailing with us this time. Who knows? Maybe in a month or two ye'll get the feeling back in yer legs. Don't give up hope on that. It's happened before to men who thought they'd never walk again."

"Maybe. I would like to see this *Enchanted Princess* you bought. You make her sound like she really is enchanted. Maybe you can scrape up some pixie dust off her deck and sprinkle it over my legs and make me well again."

Father and the captain both laughed. I did not for it seemed to me that Father's condition was no laughing matter. Perhaps I was wrong, but it seemed too severe a situation at the time. Yet, once he saw the *Enchanted Princess* and once I saw the joy on his face, I felt much better at having him go aboard.

His pride was only one of the reasons he agreed to the captain's plan. He did not want the men to pity him. If it was his lot in life to be a cripple, so be it, but he had not accepted that fate as of yet.

He had told me as much as we left the house. The other reason, he said, was because he did not want to let anyone know that 'Captain Robert' was not in full charge.

Captain Langley--for he had not yet earned his reputation and the notoriety that comes by recognition of only one's first name--was a good captain, and word spread that he was tough but fair.

O'Reily's men bowed to both he and my father and doffed their caps when I came on board.

"She's a fine ship," Father said. "She's loaded with provisions and powder?"

"Aye, sir," O'Reily said. "We're as ready as can be."

"Then you've a mission, Captain Langley. Take her out beyond the horizon, and God be with you."

"Thank ye, Captain Robert. I'll sail her true to the north star and capture that bastard Diego or die trying."

"I want my ship back. If you capture her, 'twill be two ships you'll command and all the treasure she carries. Diego would load her down so his ship would ride high and be more maneuverable in a fight."

"I'll remember that, sir. We'll not make any mistakes."

"Good. Be off with you and, Esther, you'll come back to the house with me."

"But...I thought I would be going along."

"Not this time, Missus Mountbatten," the captain said politely. "Come time for a victory sail, ye're welcome to bring Lord Mountbatten and join yer father and me. We'll fly Diego's colors and cut the line so we drags them behind in our wake. That will show everyone that the bastard is no longer a threat to English ships."

"And Smithers," Father said. "Don't forget Smithers."

"Oh, we'll offer him a hanging on the mast or a dunk in the sea, whichever he prefers."

The mood was overly joyful. I suppose that is the way of men when they set about on an adventure. In his polite way, Captain Langley had excused me from this trip and Father had allowed it.

Very well, the maiden voyage without a maiden, except of course for the wooden princess showing them the way. This would have to change because I was learning to love the sea and the crab-covered sand on the beaches. I would have an audience with Father. If he could tend to business, then it was my duty to accept that. But if he could not, then as heir to his business I would be in my rights to take over. I may be young, but it was easy to see that with men like these there needed to be better organization. What I didn't know I could learn and no better teacher than my own father.

Yes, we most certainly would have a talk.

Chapter 15
A Walk in the Garden

After seeing Father home, his driver took me to my house. Phillip met me at the door with a look of worry upon his face.

"Are you all right, my dear?" Phillip reached out and drew me to him in a warm embrace.

"Yes, of course, I just came from Father's house."

"I was worried when you didn't return last night."

"Oh, that. Captain Langley and I picked out a ship for Father—a frigate-for him to sail after the pirate, Diego."

"Yes, I know, the news is all over Portsmouth; also, that you spent the night alone on the island with your Captain Langley."

"Not alone. There were other members of the crew there."

"All men? That's even worse. You are something of a shameless hussy, especially with the reputation Captain Langley has." Phillip laughed.

"Well, you suggested I spend the day with him."

"That's what he told you?"

"Yes. Isn't that what you intended?"

"Not all night."

"Oh. I'm sorry. Have I overstepped my bounds?"

"No. Not with me. It's just talk. Everybody talks about everybody else. Don't worry about it. Did you have a good time with the captain."

"Yes. We had a wonderful sail around the southern end of Lovers' Island."

He scooped me up in his arms and carried me to the divan on the patio. We were alone. The servants had gone their separate ways.

A cool breeze blew our way and the air was fresh with the fragrance of magnolia and lavender and apple blossoms.

"I missed you so," Phillip said.

He stretched me out on the divan and began rubbing my feet like he used to do when we were children.

"Do you still enjoy this?" he asked.

"Don't stop now, my husband," I replied. I enjoyed the attention he paid me

The day flew by and we enjoyed ourselves in all the ways a newlywed couple might. I was thankful it was the servants' day off as we were quite loud and quite naughty.

Toward the evening, Phillip led me into our bedroom and handed me a rather large box.

"Take this," he said.

I opened the box and found a new light yellow chiffon dress. Low cut, but modest enough for entertaining. I hurriedly dressed as Phillip left to greet someone at the door. He returned and led me back downstairs to the study.

"She is ready, Monsieur." Phillip touched my elbow gently and guided me toward a man dressed in a white smock and black beret, a Frenchman I gathered from the way Phillip addressed him.

He was a short man with thin mustache and goatee and a smile that seemed never to leave his face.

"Pardon, Mademoiselle Mountbatten. Sit here, please. You are the daughter, no?"

"No," Phillip interrupted. "She is my wife."

"Oh, but of course. How stupid of me. Please sit so I can adjust your hair and clothing for the portrait I will paint. Such a beautiful lady you are."

He fumbled with my hair, laying the long strands over my shoulders and arranging the ringlets to drape over my breasts, which he pressed gently, maybe innocently with the backs of his hands. The shoulders of the dress could be worn up or down, and the painter tugged them over the points of my shoulders to lay sideways then very boldly tugged at the center of the blouse to expose a considerable amount of cleavage. Phillip, all the while, looked on approvingly. When I caught his eye, he did nothing but smile and nod his head.

Canvas and easel arranged, the artist showed me the painting he had already completed for Phillip. There was no doubt he was an accomplished painter, having captured Phillip's likeness to perfection. An hour later he stopped sketching my likeness and covered the canvas. He told me I could relax now.

"Can I see it?"

"Oh, no, madam...tut, tut, tut...not until she is complete. I have only captured the general image of your beautiful face. I shall finish the portrait in another five days and then you can hang both of these in your parlor."

I left them alone while I went to my bedroom and flopped across the mattress. The day's events had worn heavy on me.

Chapter 16
The *Enchanted Princess* Returns

A strong pounding sounded on our front door. The hour was late and I wondered who it might be.

Phillip opened the door whilst I remained upstairs at the balcony listening.

"We did it, yer lordship. We captured *The Neptune*. And Smithers is no longer someone Cap'n Robert has to worry about."

Captain Langley was drunk. His voice slurred when he spoke. I peeked around the corner and could see him staggering into the foyer. He held a bottle of rum in one hand and clapped Phillip on the shoulder with the other.

"That's great news, but do you know what time it is?"

"Hang the time. It's time to celebrate. Let me tell you all about it."

"Fine. Fine, but come inside and sit down. Yes, tell me all about the battle."

I tightened the thin robe around me, drawing the string belt up under my breasts and fashioning a knot. I walked down the stairs and followed them into the parlor.

Captain Langley turned as I came through the door. A broad smile covered his face and he beamed at me with eyes only slightly crossed.

"Here, take this," he handed the bottle to Phillip. "I want a kiss from Cap'n Robert's daughter."

"I think you're a bit too drunk..." Phillip stopped himself as the captain swept me up into his arms and swirled me around.

He tried to kiss me on the lips but I turned a cheek to him instead. He stopped turning about and lowered me to my feet.

"She's a lovely thing, isn't she?" He said to Phillip. "Ye're the luckiest man alive, yer lordship."

"Yes, I think so," Phillip replied. He smiled, more amused at the captain's drunken revelry than upset by his bad manners. "But the hour is late and..."

"It's all right, Phillip."

I couldn't believe I said that.

"What?"

"I said, it's all right. I'm happy the captain has rescued my father's ship. He deserves a bit of bragging."

"Well, all is fine. Captain Langley," Phillip said. "I congratulate you on your successful adventure. But, perhaps the rest of your celebration could wait until in the morning."

"Aye-aye, yer lordship."

Captain Langley snapped himself to attention and saluted Phillip, then broke into a broad smile as he began to bow.

He didn't quite complete that action. He fell face-first onto the Persian rug and began to snore loudly.

I laughed heartily at the way he landed with his face on the floor and his bottom sticking up in the air. I returned to our bedroom while Phillip dragged the captain to a divan and removed his boots. The young fool was down for the night. I lay my head on the pillow and thought back to our hero falling face down in the parlor. I was still giggling when Phillip returned to bed.

The next morning, Captain Langley—a bit ragged and fuzzy-brained from the night before—accompanied us to Father's house where he told what he could remember of his great adventure.

"We caught sight of her, sir, just off the tip before Pevensey. She was heavy laden, she was, jes' as ye figured. Diego's ship was being pressed by a French vessel. I couldn't identify her 'cept by her colors. Whilst she was occupying Diego's ship, we struck the British Jack and fired a round above her stern. She fired back and we took it high a-broadside, but there was little damage. I sent two balls in return and landed 'em high, one to yer cabin, I'm afraid, and t'other took out a longboat, but the cap'n could see we meant business so he struck his colors and we boarded her."

"Who was the captain?" Father asked.

"Some fancy dan by the name of Delahandra. I lined up all his officers and there amongst them was Smithers. First mate, he was. I gave a good little speech and he gave me a curse or two in return. I explained to the captain what a mongrel traitor Smithers was and that in time he would have done in the Spaniard first chance he got his hands on their gold."

"And what of Smithers' fate?"

"Hung him from a yardarm, I did."

"Good for you, captain." Father chuckled. "And the others?"

"I put the Spanish captain and his officers in a longboat and heaved 'em over the side. The rest of his crew I impressed into service to work the riggings. My own first mate, a right nice chap named O'Riley, took command. She's in port now sir being repaired. She's loaded down with what they took from you and more, I suspect."

"You've done well, Captain Langley. Now you have two ships and once repairs have been made you can head out again and see if Diego survived the attack. If he did, I want his head."

"Aye, aye, sir."

Father and Captain Langley talked a while longer, mostly about the repairs that were needed and the transfer of the treasure to Father's holdings. Half of that would go to the captain and his crew, but from the sound of it, Father would still have more than he had lost to Diego and, of course, *The Neptune* was his again. Father loved that ship, and I was happy for him.

Phillip was supposed to have transacted the banking for Father, but he was in a mood. That was understandable, I suppose, after the way Father praised and rewarded Captain Langley. I contacted the bank myself and had them make an inventory to determine how much would go to Father, and how much would be set aside in a new account for Captain Trevor Langley, Esquire. Our young captain would like the sound of that. From thief to a gentleman of the sea in less than six months, he had improved himself quite nicely. In time, he would be expected to marry. I wasn't sure I liked that idea since I was still having girlish romantic notions about him; shameful, of course, because I was a married woman. I seriously chided myself because Phillip was a good provider and I always had Father to help. My worldly position was secure so I should not have such stray thoughts. It was a time when I could enjoy myself and so I busied the days ahead with filling my social calendar.

My first party included Count Armand of Selsey and the Countess and Lord and Lady Covington. I did this not because I particularly cared for any of them but because I thought it would be fun to have the count drool over me and to see how Lady Covington reacted in front of Captain Langley with her husband so close at hand.

I didn't wish any secrets to come out or for anyone to be embarrassed or hurt, I just enjoyed the idea of knowing secrets and watching how the people with them would react to one another.

The party went well and, as predicted, I found myself in a corner with Count Armand still wanting me and plying me with sweet talk.

"Count Armand," I whispered so no one else could hear, "I'm not a little innocent virgin anymore."

"You are a very beautiful lady," he replied. "Your deflowering brings out a light in your face and a glow to your bosom."

"And you would like to bask in that glow, I gather."

"Oh, madam, if you would only consider such...I would be the happiest man at the party."

I laughed at him and excused myself. There was no way I would ever let him know me carnally but I was in such a mischievous spirit I enjoyed my little game of teasing him.

I rejoined the party and made straightway for Phillip who was having a lively conversation with the Countess. I ran my palm across Phillips face and allowed him to kiss it before shaking hands with the Countess.

"By any chance, have you seen my husband?" She asked.

"I spoke with him a few minutes ago." I smiled. "But he left to get some fresh air, I think."

"Oh, excuse me, then. I shall go and find him. You look so lovely in that gown my dear. Green is becoming to you."

"Thank you. This is one of my husband's favorite gowns."

The Countess left us and Phillip grabbed my arm a little tighter. "What kind of foolishness are you up to? Were you playing with the Count's passions, my little minx? And what's all this about that being my favorite gown?"

"Well, it is the gown you bought me especially for this party, is it not? Oh, I see Aunt Eller approaching."

"Hello, Mother." Phillip kissed her hand.

"Aunt Eller, how nice to see you. Are you enjoying yourself?"

"Oh, yes, 'tis a grand party. You two look so adorable."

"Aunt Eller, there is something I want to get your opinion on. Women's talk,"

I unhooked my arm from Phillip's and led Aunt Eller away to speak quietly.

"Aunt Eller, how well do you know the captain which Father has hired to command his ships?"

She paused for a moment to catch her breath. When she looked at me, I could see a question in her eyes.

"I have seen him out and about in Portsmouth."

"Did you know that he was the thief that stole my necklace that night the British troops came to our home?"

"Oh." Her sharp intake of air silenced her.

"Well, he was. And I have heard a strange story about him that perhaps you and he were more than just acquainted."

"Oh, no." She dropped her shoulders and grabbed her chest. I thought I might have gone too far, but she was still quite young, only forty-two, so I did not think she was in ill health. "Esther, I..."

"It's all right, Aunt Eller. I know the story is true. He told me."

Aunt Eller looked at me for a moment.

"Oh, my dear. You have grown so much. But I warned you about men like him, and him in particular. I pray you have not fallen for his charms."

"No. Not yet, auntie; not in any carnal way. I'm just curious why so many women find him so attractive."

"Well, he is a charmer," she admitted. "He is also a bit of a scoundrel and most definitely has a dark, brooding side to him at times. I suppose all women find his kind of danger to be appealing."

"You know, 'tis said he has had just about every woman in Portsmouth, some more than once."

"Yes, I know. He has bragged of his conquests, but he does not do that in public. I feel very safe in my reputation. Ours was only a one-time dalliance. Please say nothing to my son about this. I'm sure he believes that all women are either virtuous or whores and a wide gap exists between the two."

"As I said, this is women's talk. Your secret is safe with me."

Changing the subject I said, "Did you know I invited Lady Covington and her husband here tonight?"

"You didn't?"

"I did."

"You naughty little wench," Aunt Eller pinched my arm. "You know he's had her, and her husband doesn't know."

"Well, I shan't be the one to tell him. I simply wanted to see the look on her face when she comes face to face with him."

"From what I'm told, she didn't have her face toward him when last they met."

"Oh, Aunt Eller, how funny you are."

"There are men born to be lovers and men who can love and deserve to be loved. I war you again not to fall under the captain's spell. Love my son, your husband, for who and what he is and try not to hurt him by letting him think you favor the captain."

I left my aunt and introduced Captain Langley to Lord and Lady Covington. The two men got along greatly whilst Lady Covington retreated so her husband would not see her blush so.

The captain smiled wickedly at her when her husband was not looking, which caused her to blush even more. I faded into the background to enjoy the little show they were putting on without realizing that they were all actors and I was their stage director.

There is little worth repeating in the things they had to say. Satisfied with my little game, I moved swiftly amongst my guests bidding them have fun, eat, drink and be merry as the saying goes.

All in all, everyone seemed to have a wonderful time. Eventually the guests all left. As a final gesture of hijinks on my part, I asked Captain Langley if he would escort Aunt Eller back to Father's house. I winked at Aunt Eller as they entered Phillip's carriage.

The last guest having left, I turned to Phillip and suggested we go to bed. Neither of us seemed in need of sleep and I had other things on my mind. I had been a little hard on Phillip, now it was time to show him how much I wanted him. He could be the aggressor and I his willing, submissive wife. Tonight Phillip would have the upper hand, and I wasted no time once we were in the bedroom in showing him just how willing I was to be his.

Chapter 17
Plans of Our Own

With the sunrise, Phillip and I got dressed before Alice served us breakfast in the garden. Alice was a little closed-mouthed around me, not at all like when we first met, but she smiled at Phillip as she served him, then excused herself so that we might eat and talk alone.

"You were pretty good last night," I told him.

"Pretty good? Just pretty good?"

"You are good." I laughed at his mock worry.

"I suppose I should take some happiness in that if that is all I can get out of you this morning."

"My darling husband, we have always loved one another and I think I should never see a day that I would not love you."

"I missed you while you spent all night long on the Isle of Wight with all those men."

I laughed again because Phillip was making a pouty face.

"I did nothing but sleep whilst Captain Langley and O'Riley talked all night about a strange rock they had found. There must be a treasure buried on the island and our good and loyal captain seems to know where it is."

"There have always been stories about buried pirate treasure on the island. And if there is, I'm not sure we should trust our 'good and loyal captain' to deliver it to us. What makes him think he knows where it is?"

I told Phillip about the locket and how Captain Langley had been the thief who had stolen it from me. It seemed to convince him that the treasure was real and no doubt reinforced his suspicion of the man's integrity.

"If you could get your hands on that locket, you and I could go back and look for it ourselves. Captain Langley has enough gold that he took when he recaptured *The Neptune*. It was your necklace to begin with, it should be your find and your fortune, whatever it might be."

"You raise an interesting point, my husband. Perhaps we should raise a crew of our own and go in search of this treasure."

"How soon before he takes to sea again?"

"Oh, I think they are still celebrating their booty. I'm sure he will not go out again until repairs are made for both ships."

"Then we should move swiftly. Let us get through today's labors and make our plans this evening."

We rode into the orchards later that day and observed that all was going well. Phillip's apple trees were bountiful and the pickers were taking bushels from each tree, nice ripe ruby red apples with glistening skins that reflected the sun's rays as if each of them were polished mirrors. We rode among the workers observing until we came across a muscular lad early in his twenties.

"Daniel," my husband called to him.

"G'morning, sir. Madam." He tipped his straw hat in my direction.

"Esther, may I present Daniel Thornberry, the son of a dear friend of mine. Daniel, didn't you tell me you once served on a ship?"

"Aye, sir. I was cabin boy aboard a frigate out of Dublin.

"Do you know how to sail, then?"

"Hmm, maybe a small ship."

"Would you like to go down to the pier and pick us out a schooner and check the pier and pubs for a crew, all sturdy men such as yourself?"

"Aye, sir. Where will be sailing to?"

"Just tell the men it will be up and down the coast on a fishing voyage."

"Fishing, from a schooner?"

"Nothing commercial."

"No, I don't think you'd be making a profit. If it is for pleasure, then may I ask why that size of a ship and not a sloop?"

Phillip leaned over his horse and in a quieter tone so others would not hear, "Daniel, I have my reasons and they are not to be discussed."

"Sorry, sir. Your business is yours, my business is to take orders from you. Shall I leave right away?"

"Yes, stop what you are doing and climb aboard my wife's horse. We'll carry you back."

Phillip pulled me up behind him so Daniel could take my horse. We rode to Portsmouth at a fine clip. We reached the merchant's bank and the boy slid quickly off the back of my horse, handing the reins to me.

Tethering the horses to a post, I followed as Daniel and Phillip went inside to arrange a sum of funds from which this suddenly promoted captain could draw as he pleased to purchase and outfit a ship.

After that, Phillip bid him farewell and we returned home.

"I assume you trust him," I said.

"With everything I own," Phillip said. "As I said, he's the son of a dear friend." He quickly changed the subject. "You know, I fancy an afternoon nap, don't you?"

"I believe that would do nicely."

We mounted the stairs to our bedroom after leaving word with Alice that we should not be disturbed. She nodded and removed herself from our presence. Phillip closed the door as I began undressing. I'm afraid we didn't get much sleep at all.

Chapter 18
Plans Are Made

Phillip answered the door himself. Daniel stood there with a broad smile on his face. He entered at my husband's welcome and Phillip ushered him into the parlor. I joined them and listened intently as the young man told my husband about the purchase.

"I have a crew loading it now," he said.

"Can you sail it?"

"Yes, sir. If all we do is sail up and down the coast, I can handle it. If bad weather comes, it will be more up to the men than it will me, but I do know these waters and there is little chance of running aground even in bad weather. It depends, of course, on how bad the winds blow."

"Well, we're not into the heavy storm season, yet, so we should have some luck with the weather. Let me tell you where you are going."

Phillip quickly briefed Daniel about Lover's Island and what we hoped to find there. He cautioned him to be quiet and the young man swore himself to secrecy.

Phillip excused himself to use the privy.

When we were alone, Daniel said, "I know you, don't I?"

"I am the daughter of Captain Robert, a buccaneer. He is brother to Phillip's mother."

The Buccaneer's Daughter

We talked about family and our stations in life until Phillip returned. They went over their plans again and I found it quite boring to rehash all the details so I excused myself and retired to our bedroom. Daniel took his leave sometime during the night.

To say that we had a plan would be stretching things a bit. Other than ensuring that each man was armed and that there were proper provisions on board we at least thought to add implements such as picks and shovels, rope, and poles.

The only thing not readily available to us was the heart shaped necklace Captain Langley had taken from me the night we met, the one he had showed to O'Riley at the painted rock. It fell to me to try and fetch it. We reasoned that the captain would not keep the locket upon himself, but put it in a safe place where he could reach it at a moment's notice. That meant, for want of a better idea, that he had it in the captain's cabin on board ship. But which ship, *The Neptune* or the *Enchanted Princess*? After careful consideration, we decided that since he commanded *The Neptune*, that must be where he kept it. The idea was unthinkable that he should trust someone else with its safekeeping. I approached *The Neptune* and spoke with McGinty, small talk to win his confidence, then the contrived story that Father had asked me to look in his cabin to see if his favorite book had survived the changing of hands from him to Smithers to Captain Langley.

McGinty was, of course, a little bit cautious but since I was Captain Robert's daughter and since the ship belonged to Father, I was allowed to enter the cabin and search it.

I did so with extreme care and much haste. After prodding through Father's desk and in various cubbyholes, I found the necklace in the strangest of places, wrapped around the base of the oil lamp hanging from the ceiling arch. I carefully unwrapped it and pocketed it, then grabbed a book from Father's shelf and stepped out of the cabin.

"And did ye find what ye needed, ma'am?"

"Yes, I have it right here." I held the book up for McGinty to see. He read the title on its cover and looked at me curiously.

"I dinny think yer father was a religious man."

I looked at the book and saw it was a Bible. If Father was known for being a saint, it certainly wasn't around Portsmouth. More sinner than saint, at least he had a reputation for being an educated man.

"My father reads everything that is committed to print. He feels if there is a thought worthy of going to press, then it is worthy of his time to study it."

"I see," McGinty studied me carefully, not at all appearing convinced of my story. "Well, ye have what ye came for. G'night, m'lady."

"Good night, Mister McGinty." I quickly shot down the gangplank and out of sight to where Phillip and Daniel were waiting.

"Did you get it?" Phillip asked.

"The locket is safe," I said, touching my breasts to indicate that I was now wearing it.

"We'd best be off," Daniel said. "There are men milling about, some of them may work for your father."

"You mean for Captain Langley."

"Whichever," Phillip interrupted, "Daniel is right. We need to move."

The three of us found our way to the schooner Daniel had obtained. We boarded and the crew pulled out of port silently. There was a good wind that carried us away from the harbor and set us on course for the Isle of Wight.

"We'll get there about three o'clock," Daniel said. "We'll stay on board until first light. No way of telling what kind of animals come out at night, and with us going into the bush I'd just as soon be able to see them as well as they can see us."

"You're worried about furry creatures?" I asked.

"Them and the two-legged ones with guns and swords," he said.

We dropped anchor near where I had stopped on my first trip to the island. The breeze was cool and I found a comfortable place to rest until morning. We had no light aboard, not wanting to signal our presence to anyone. It was doubtful that we should meet anyone but felt it was safer to lay in total darkness. With the early morning light we went ashore with tools, food and all the crew except for two remaining on board as watchers.

"The rock?" Phillip asked.

"This way, see the tracks are still clear."

We made our way through the trees to the painted rock. Daniel held a lantern up to read the inscriptions whilst I presented the locket opened as I had seen Captain Langley do. I closed the locket as he had done and the arrow that decorated it pointed to our right.

"How far?" Phillip asked.

"The captain didn't say," I replied.

"Look," said Daniel. "The feathers on the arrow are different. There are four carvings above and three below. I wonder if that is come kind of clue?"

"Could be," Phillip said, "I suppose we think in terms of distance. Four feet to our right, three feet beneath the surface."

"That makes sense," Daniel said.

We saw a large boulder four feet from where we stood. The crew rolled it out of the way and broke out the shovels. By the time the sun rose over the horizon, one of the crew struck something buried within the sandy loam.

"A box!" one of the men cried out.

"The treasure!" They all beamed.

"Dig it up," another voice called out. It was a voice I recognized right away. I turned and looked at Captain Langley's face, bearing a broad grin. Behind him stood O'Riley, who was holding a blunderbuss. "Ye saved me a lot of work, Lady Esther. I only wish ye had trusted me enough to share a bit of it with me."

"This is Father's treasure," I said, defiantly.

"Well, it belongs to whoever finds it…or whoever can hold onto it."

"You have us at your mercy, it seems," Phillip said.

He stood between the captain and me and stared at O'Riley, who had lifted the blunderbuss.

"No need for that, my good man. As you can see we are unarmed except for pick and shovel."

The captain waved his hand toward O'Riley who dropped the barrel of his weapon. That gave Phillip the edge he, no doubt, had sought. He pulled a pistol from his waistcoat and fired point blank at O'Riley. The Irishman yelled in pain, then dropped the blunderbuss and clasped both his hands around his neck. A pulsating stream of blood shot forth from between his fingers and he dropped to the ground, moaning and kicking until he died.

Meanwhile, Daniel had also pulled out a pistol and had jumped the distance of about four feet to reach the captain. Daniel jammed the pistol into the man's ribs and cocked the hammer.

"I wouldn't move if I were you."

"The thought never crossed my mind." The captain's mustache rose at the corners of his mouth and his teeth glistened in the sunlight. "I didn't see your pistols in time. I'm afraid."

"What shall we do with him?" Daniel asked.

"Bind him and be on the lookout for the rest of his crew."

"That won't be necessary," Captain Langley said. "I came with O'Riley and one other who is back on our boat."

"Check it out," Daniel told one of our men. The sailor armed himself and crept through the bushes.

He returned in a moment in a fit of worry.

"He's telling the truth, sir. But we've even more danger waiting. There be a full-sized Man-O-War sitting in the bay, and she's flying the skull and bones."

"Diego!" Captain Langley said. "Quick, cut me loose. Together we might stand a chance."

Daniel looked at Phillip, who had a look of anguish on his face.

"Hurry, for God's sake," the captain hissed.

"No," I said. "Quickly, fill in the sand, cover the treasure."

"What are you saying?" Phillip asked.

"Listen to me. I know what I am doing. Cover the spot where the treasure is buried and roll the stone another ten feet away. If Diego knows about the treasure, he will know it is buried under the rock. Move the rock and he will spend hours looking for it. We'll take a circular path to our ships and set sail for Portsmouth and pick up the crews from *The Neptune* and the *Enchanted Princess*. We come back here, seize Diego's ship whilst he is busy looking for the treasure. We capture him, his ship, and take the treasure to boot."

"She's brilliant!" Captain Langley said.

"I agree," Daniel seconded.

"As do I. You heard her, men, make haste," Phillip commanded.

Having hidden O'Reilly's body and brushed our trail with branches, judging that the rock looked like it had been there a long time, we melted into the underbrush. Behind us, we could hear the footsteps of men approaching the spot where the rock could be found. When the footsteps stopped, we figured they had reached the spot. Moving swiftly, we broke the tree line just down the beach and found our skiffs were still moored in the water a goodly distance from Diego's ship. He had not assigned any of his crew to keep watch on them. We rowed silently out to our schooner and another one Captain Langley had used, and as quietly as possible we weighed anchor and let the ship drift with the tide until we were out of rifle range. Then we hoisted sail and turned both ships toward Portsmouth. Luckily, Diego's men never tried to stop us.

Chapter 19
To Arms, To Arms

McGinty, being a quick-minded man, took the helm of *The Neptune* and rousted the crew to battle stations. Phillip sailed with him to give directions. Daniel and I took command of the *Enchanted Princess*. I took Captain Langley with me, still a prisoner, but I figured if the fighting got too heavy his knowledge of battle would come in handy. I had the idea he would not let me be harmed if things went badly.

Daniel took over as first mate and the crew obliged him. He knew enough about ships to get us underway.

"Have ye ever been in battle?" Captain Langley asked.

"One," Daniel answered. "Once was enough, I thought, but if it has to be..."

"Can ye use a cutlass?"

"Aye, that I can. And before you ask your next question, captain, yes, I've killed before."

This came as a shock to me, for I found Daniel to be such a gentle sort. I hoped now that he had fury enough to do well in battle, should we have to fight. I was hoping we wouldn't have to fight, hoping that Diego was still on the island looking for the treasure whilst we commandeered his ship.

The Buccaneer's Daughter

We arrived back at the island just as the sun was setting. That was fortunate for us since we were coming in from the eastern side of the island, round its tip. The approaching darkness hid our approach until we were almost upon her. Diego's men had taken the moment to go swimming, fishing or exploring the silvery sands of the beach. Their attention taken by so many diversions we were able to slip alongside and drop anchor. Not until we tossed our grappling hooks and swung over did the Spaniards realize they were under attack.

I looked at Captain Langley, who begged to be cut loose. I don't think he was concerned about anything but the fight. Being the man he was, he wanted to swing his cutlass and draw blood.

I was beginning to see him in a new light. As much of a preening cock as he was, I saw him for the kind of man he was inside and perhaps not someone I would want around me anymore. Nevertheless, when all of this was over I vowed to talk to Father about letting him go.

I had not planned on joining in the fighting myself. After all, I was only a female and barely eighteen at that, not what you'd expect to see in a fight against a bunch of mean old pirates.

That choice, however, was not mine to make. As our crew fought heartily, quickly overpowering those on Diego's ship, some of his men had gone over the side and now had climbed the anchor chain at the bow of the *Enchanted Princess*. Only one other sailor and I had remained on board to guard our prisoner. The sailor spotted the two

Spaniards as they topped the rail and headed our way.

"Cut me loose," the captain pleaded.

I was about to do that when the first one cornered the crewmember and the second one leaped down in front of me. I raised my pistol and his eyes widened then he smiled, thinking I'm sure that he had nothing to fear from a mere girl. He brandished two swords and swung them in circular motions moving the blades left and right as he approached.

I shot him. The blue powder flew out of the end of the barrel so thick that at first I couldn't tell whether or not I had hit him. He staggered back, but that could have been out of fear. Yet, when the haze of smoke cleared I could clearly see the puncture wound in his upper chest and the blood trailing from it.

The impact had caused him to drop one of his cutlasses. He still held the other one in his hand and he lifted it high above his head as he regained his balance and stared at me with a mean and deathly look. I grabbed his other sword, since the pistol had only been a single shot and I wasn't sure I could reload it in time. The pirate swung his cutlass in a downward arch and I moved to the side, blocking it with the one I held. The blades rang in that metallic sound they make and he swung upwards, aiming at my head. All of the lessons Father had taught me came to mind and I again managed to block the man's assault. As his sword glanced upwards off mine, I thrust forward and opened a gash along his bicep. He stopped and

I took advantage of his sudden lack of control. I swung my sword upwards in a long arch, which left a rather satisfying mark across his chest.

He jumped back at the attack and had a surprised look on his face. The wound in his chest was bleeding a steady stream and he must have grown weak from it, because he did not move quickly. He raised his blade, aiming it at my throat, but I ducked and lunged forward, plunging my own blade through his midsection. He hung there on my blade and dropped his own sword. I raised a foot and kicked him hard enough to send him flying. As luck would have it, he fell against his own man, which took the advantage away from him and my crewman ended the fight much the same way as I had by sticking the man with the sword he had.

Over on Diego's ship, a roar of victory filled the air. I was unsure as to which side had won until Daniel swung back over to the *Enchanted Princess*, a big smile on his face.

"We did it!" he yelled. "We beat the bloodiest pirate in the English Channel. Well, he wasn't on board, but that doesn't matter. We have his ship."

"I suppose he's still on the island," I said.

"Then we'll leave him there for the magistrate to deal with. We now have three ships ... and one traitorous bastard to deal with." Daniel stepped in front of Trevor and raised his cutlass. The blade was still heavy with Spanish blood on it. "What say you, Lady Esther? You are our captain. Shall I rid us of this miserable cur swiftly or have him walk the plank?"

"No." I couldn't let Daniel simply kill the man. I suppose I had the right. Oh, my gosh, Daniel had proclaimed me captain--not Phillip. Yes, I had the right to administer justice; after all, Captain Langley and his man O'Riley had approached us on the island under arms. It was quite possible they would have killed us to keep the treasure to themselves. "No. We'll take him before Father and let him decide. These are still his ships, not mine."

"Aye-aye, captain. Whatever you say."

Phillip swung over the side to see how I had fared. I told him about the two Spaniards who had attacked us and called the sailor over to thank him. Phillip shook his hand and promised him a bonus when we returned. He stood in front of our prisoner, who smirked at the damage that had been done to Phillip's clothing; it was torn and covered in blood.

"Aren't ye the sight, Mister High-and-Mighty. Ye can't protect yer own lady..."

The captain never got to finish his taunting. Phillip swung a hard fist that smashed against his cheek and sent him sprawling to the deck. When he tried to stand, his mouth was bloody and one of his teeth had been knocked out. It lay there stuck to his lip.

"Right nice punch, I'd say. O'course, if me hands were untied ye'd never have gotten the hit."

"I feel so sorry for you," Phillip said and turned his back on the man.

"Daniel, will you take command of the Spanish vessel? There's an officer over there who will sail it for you in exchange for his life. Just look after the prisoners until we get into Portsmouth."

"Uh, that will be fine with me if it's fine with the captain," Daniel said, looking straight at me."

"You called my wife captain."

"Rule of the sea. A ship's crew can name its own captain, sir."

Phillip looked at me with a new light of interest in his eyes.

"I suppose you have shown yourself to be a leader this day. Very well, you are the captain, my dear. What are your orders?"

"The same as yours, my husband. We are a team."

Daniel excused himself as more of the crew returned to the ship.

I took to the rigging so all three ships could see me. Waving my arm in the direction of Portsmouth, all three ships turned about and we headed for home.

In the distance, just before we got turned about fully, I could see Diego and a handful of his men break the tree line and run toward the beach.

I could see, too, that he was empty handed. He had not found the treasure. That meant another trip to the island after some rest for the men and some celebration.

Father would be pleased to see us and to find out that we had so insulted the great Spanish pirate.

Diego still had a longboat, the one he'd used to go ashore. I knew he wouldn't be on the island when we returned. A shame, really. I would have liked to capture him as well and present him to Father and then to the magistrate. Capturing his ship would have to do.

Chapter 20
Father's Comments

Captain Langley's arms were still bound as we marched him into Father's bedroom. We relayed the story as accurately as possible. The captain had nothing to say until Father asked him pointblank, "Did you plan to steal the treasure and do harm to my daughter and crew?"

"Well, sir, the treasure was up for grabs, I reckoned. As for doing harm to yer daughter, I wouldn't be harmin' a hair on her head. We've formed a sort of special relationship, ye see." He lied, of course. Even captured he seemed to want to play the part of a rogue.

Father waved him to silence. The look in Father's eyes was enough to warn him that any further comment could cost him his life. The fool was not a man to be afraid of anyone, but even with Father being crippled, the beast could not look him in the eye.

"You worked for me." Father admonished him. "Any treasure taken while you were under my sail and my flag belongs to the company."

Father sat up more in bed and continued admonishing Captain Langley.

"You would have received an honest share, as would each of the crew. That's the buccaneer way. Any private venture is the same as taking food from my mouth. If I had been in command on board the ship, you would have received thirty lashes with a cat of nine tails."

"I ask yer forgiveness, Cap'n Robert."

"I do not give it." Father's voice came in a surly and sour note. His eyes burned with hatred. A captain demands loyalty from his crew; any sailor not showing loyalty to his captain and to the ship is as useless as tits on a boar hog. "You have strayed over the line, Captain Langley. If you know what's good for you, you'll keep your peace and live out your sentence. Magistrate, take him away."

"Aye, Captain Robert. We'll see how he fares with Her Majesty's court."

"Not very well, I should think." Captain Langley's last words trailed away as the magistrate dragged him from the room.

"Now, what have we to discuss?" Father asked.

"Sir," Phillip spoke first. "We have *The Neptune*, the *Enchanted Princess*, and Diego's ship, the *Spanish Lady*. We have recovered your original holdings, plus what Diego and Smithers had taken from other ships and Diego's own ship was heavy with jewels and fine china and silk. We haven't yet tallied the new take but it is considerable."

Father thought for a minute, rubbed his hand across his graying beard and looked Phillip square in the eye.

"And you think there's still treasure buried on the island?" he asked.

"Aye, sir," Daniel spoke. "And we're ready to claim it soon as the captain gives us her word."

"*Her* word?"

"The men have rallied around Esther and chosen her as their leader," Phillip explained. "I must admit, she has been the driving force behind gaining the ships and finding the treasure on the island."

"But you said you rolled the marking rock well away from where you had found the treasure. Can you find it again, daughter?"

"Yes, Father. If you approve of me leading the party."

"Who am I to go against three whole crews bound to serve under you. Phillip can go if he pleases. For the business of this family, he still runs the store and orchards but you can sail the ships as you please. I will teach you what I know of sailing and I'm sure the crews will fit a sail as you command."

"Sir, each man would lay down his life for her," Daniel said.

"So be it. Allow me the pleasure of enjoying your adventures each time you come to port. Bring me something pretty and shiny and thrill me with your deeds of derring-do."

"I shall tell you wonderful stories about how we hunt the Spaniards and French and how we vex them without mercy," I said to my loving father.

"Good. But all things tomorrow. Tonight we must celebrate." He turned to face Daniel and ordered, "Young man, have some of the crew break out a couple of kegs and set them up in the garden. Sister Eller, have the cook prepare a feast."

Aunt Eller had been in the room all along, but as always she had kept her tongue. Now she spoke, "My brother, earlier in the day I had already instructed the cook to put a pig on the spit. It will be done in time for the merriment."

"Is this a lovely family or what?"

Father was extremely pleased with the way things had turned out. We celebrated all that night until the next morning just before the cock crowed its first cock-a-doodle-doo.

Later, Father called me to his bedside privately to ask me about Captain Langley.

"He will try to cause trouble for you once he is released from prison," Father said.

"I do not think so, Father."

"Oh, and why shouldn't he? After all, he will spend a considerable amount of time behind bars for what he has done."

"I wanted to talk to you about that. Am I truly in charge, Father?"

"Well, yes, seeing as how the crew wants it that way."

"No, I don't just mean on the high seas. I mean everything."

"Well, Phillip does have considerable knowledge and he is quite adept at running the store to sell what we take in."

"I'm not competing with my husband, Father. What's his is mine and what's mine is his. I'm talking about taking your place. You know I love you so and I know how hard it must be for you to let go…but…oh, Father, that bastard Diego hurt you so…you can't run the business anymore."

"Esther, Esther. Hush, child. First, it was Smithers and not Diego who actually ordered the beatings. Diego is at fault only because he allowed it to happen. So, piss on him for losing his ship, Ha! But the truth is, I'm so very, very tired. I welcome the rest. You will quickly learn, my child, that being in command is a heavy responsibility. You are lucky to have such a wonderful husband to help you"

Father lay back on his pillow and rubbed his eyes.

I drew a breath and approached him and spoke in a conspiratorial voice.

"Ah, yes, but if you will not oppose me on this, and do remember that it was me and not you staring at his man's blunderbuss, I have a plan for Captain Langley."

"Oh, and what is that if I may ask?" Father looked at me curiously.

"You may, and I think you will like it. First, the magistrate owes us some favors, I believe, having rid these waters of Diego as we did."

"At least for the moment. Diego's a crafty sort, and no doubt will be under sail in another ship by the time this conversation is over."

"Precisely. But all things good in time. I want you to ask the magistrate to allow Captain Langley…to escape."

"What? He threatened you and would have stolen from me while in my employ. Not on your life…Why?"

"Curious, are you? First, he's a turncoat, but he is English. I think he genuinely loves the Queen. What he loves more is money."

"Gold doubloons and pieces of eight..." Father sang the words with a smile on his face.

"Precisely. Before the soldiers took him to jail I slipped a note to him that if he keeps his mouth shut I would reward him with gold and with his freedom."

"Clever girl. You're beginning to remind me of someone...*me*."

"If you can get the magistrate to go along with it, to free Captain Langley, I will give him enough money to make good his absence from Portsmouth and to have him approach Diego."

"To work for that scoundrel?"

I could see that Father's anger had risen again. "Yes, but working for me at the same time. He would be our double agent."

"Do you think it would work?"

"Yes, of course. Diego's men know that Captain Langley was our prisoner. Those on the *Spanish Lady* who could look down at our smaller ship and see that he was bound to the railing around the wheel housing will surely vouch for him. He is good with a ship's crew and Diego needs experienced men, especially since he lost Smithers. He needs someone who knows these waters."

A smile crept across Father's face. He understood what I wanted and nodded his head in agreement.

"So he will give us notice when Diego hunts our merchant ships and will help foil the Spaniard's plans."

"See. I told you you'd like my plan."

"You were born to be a buccaneer, my princess. You were born to lead. I'll talk to the magistrate in the late evening after he's had food to fill his fat belly and drink to put him in the best of spirits. He will find some technicality to free Captain Langley."

"Better to let him escape," I said, almost in a conniving whisper. "It will help his reputation when he approaches Diego." Father smiled at that, but I could see he was getting weaker the longer we talked. "Time for you to get some rest, Father. I have to go and find my husband and tell him what to expect."

"Aye, keep him well informed. He may not know the high seas, but he is a good person to test out your thoughts for you before you go off half-cocked."

"Rest, Father. I'll see you later."

I kissed his cheek and patted his hand. I was elated. Father had more or less declared me in total control of the family business, at least the skullduggery part of it, and I fully believed I was up to the task.

But all that could wait.

Tonight we celebrate.

"There you are, my dear," Phillip grabbed me as I stepped down the winding staircase to the open foyer. "Are you looking for a little fun?"

"Well, if I'm the captain shouldn't I be here with my men?"

"Say no more, my dear. This is your night to celebrate."

My husband pulled me tight against him and kissed me hard on the lips.

I could taste the wine and wondered how much drink he'd already consumed. He grabbed my bustle and moved it out of the way so he could grip my fanny more firmly.

"Phillip, you are such a crude bastard. How did someone born to nobility get so vulgar?"

"You'd better ask my mother that question. I do believe she chose unwisely someone other than my dearly departed father to actually plant the seed in her for me. Who knows whose blood I have running through my veins? I'm just happy we have title and money enough for you and I to live as well as we do."

"Hmmm, I've never asked you this, but since you lived such a raunchy life so far, tell me the truth—have you a mistress to tend to your needs?"

"Honestly? Yes, I do. But know this, she is no threat to you. She knows her place. She might get a little huffy once in a while, every woman gets jealous, even the mistress against the lady of the manor."

"Alice?"

"I think it best that I don't say. You have no worry of any sort. I have loved you since we were children and I will always want to be your husband, no matter how many affairs I've had…or that you have if you someday wish that, but you must always be honest with me and tell me all the juicy details."

"Perish the thought. I think you've had too much to drink already."

"Aw, but it is a night for celebration, is it not?"

Chapter 21
Return to the Island

The sun came up smiling on Portsmouth, bathing it in a warm orange glow. We arrived at the docks ready to board. McGinty had already called for the crew to stand by to attention since this was the first time they were to sail under a new captain; officially, that is.

"Permission to come aboard, Mister McGinty," I called from the railing at the top of the gangplank.

"Permission granted, welcome aboard, Captain Esther."

As I stepped one foot off the gangplank and onto the deck of *The Neptune*, the boatswain piped me aboard. A shiver went through my body. Such a thrill to be sailing my father's ship under my first command. The boatswain hit the last high note and I almost wet my underpants.

"Cap'n on board!" McGinty yelled and the entire crew snapped to attention and saluted me. I returned the salute and took my place near the wheel beside my first mate.

"Well, I've seen you safely aboard, captain. I'll be leaving you now to take my place on the *Enchanted Princess*."

"Very, well, Captain Thornberry."

Daniel left and McGinty offered me the wheel.

"Nay, take her out, Mister McGinty."

"Aye-aye, cap'n."

We sailed out of the harbor, *The Neptune* in the lead with the *Enchanted Princess* following in her wake.

"Mister McGinty, does it bother you that I did not hand over command of the *Enchanted Princess* to you? You are much more experience a sailor than Captain Thornberry."

"Beggin' yer pardon, cap'n... I suppose ye have yer reasons. I know that young Captain Thornberry is someone of importance to ye and his lordship, yer husband."

"True, but that's not the entire reason for my action. You will agree that Captain Thornberry proved himself in battle?"

"Aye, thar's no doubt he's a brave lad, as brave as any I would say."

"He has strong leadership qualities, as do you, Mister McGinty. Having to choose which man I would rather have at my side during a fight, and likewise, which man I would rather have taking charge of my father's main ship, I choose you over Captain Thornberry. I may be captain, but I could no more steer this ship out of harm's way than could the cabin boy. Do we even have a cabin boy? No matter, the truth is your captain may lead by her wits but not by her knowledge of the sea. Mister McGinty, I want you to think of *The Neptune* as your own. I'll pick and choose what battles we fight, but when there's squalls at sea, when Neptune himself rises up to claim his namesake vessel, you are the one in charge."

"An' that proves we made the right decision in picking ye for cap'n. Ye're a smart one, yer ladyship. I'm pleased to be serving under ye. I shall steer yer father's ship through still waters or the devil's own whirlpool, ma'am. An' if I may say so, with all due respect to Cap'n Robert...*The Neptune* and the other ships...they be not yer father's ships anymore. They belong to ye alone, cap'n. We sail for ye and only for ye."

"Your loyalty will be remembered and amply rewarded, Mister McGinty."

"Jes' ye be careful, cap'n. I wouldn't want to be entering yer cabin again to save ye from one of the crew."

"That was you?"

I was shocked. I had not guessed that it was McGinty that night who pulled the lecherous old sailor off of me and dropped him overboard.

"I had no idea who 'twas."

"Aye, 'twas me. I only tell ye that so ye'll know that I serves ye full well and honorably. If ye're in danger ever again, I'd lay me down and dee for ye."

"Mister McGinty, I'm overwhelmed. What can I ever do to repay you?"

"Be a good cap'n to the crew and that's payment enough. Besides, an' I mean no disrespect...seein' ye there by the moonlight was payment enough for these old eyes."

"Mister McGinty!"

"Sorry, ma'am. I shouldn't have said that."

"Mister McGinty, I'm not ashamed that you saw me naked. You've shown me nothing but respect. I believe you and I are going to get along very well."

"Recon so, ma'am. I fancy that we will have many good days ahead of us at Diego's expense, I trust."

McGinty stood up and saluted. I thought it was quite funny and laughed. Strange, strange man.

"Land ho," the sailor in the crow's nest called down to us.

I took the wheel and corrected our course, heading us into the wind.

"Lower sails," I ordered and set *The Neptune* so the tide would carry us to the southern beach where we'd weighed anchor the last time. Following us, Daniel did the same thing and the *Enchanted Princess* caught the tide water as well.

"So, are ye sure we can find the treasure again, cap'n?"

"Yes, Mister McGinty. I know right where to look."

"An' ye're not about to say until we gets in the right spot, eh?"

"Would you give away all your secrets, Mister McGinty?"

"I wouldn't trust a bleedin' soul aboard this ship. But ye can trust me, cap'n."

"I do, Mister McGinty. I trust you and the *Princess'* first mate will organize enough men and implements to dig up whatever it is and haul it back to the other ship."

"I'm forever yer loyal servant, ma'am."

McGinty made a mock bow and I giggled like a schoolgirl. This was going to be fun. I had two ships to play with, a whole gaggle of gents to order around, and a surprise waiting for me just three feet below the sandy beach. Best of all, it was Diego's treasure I was about to claim. I wish I had brought his Man-o-War, but the truth is neither Daniel nor I could have piloted such vessel—McGinty maybe, but I needed his experience with me even though I was used to *The Neptune*.

It had to be the smaller ship, the *Enchanted Princess*, so Daniel could handle it.

Being captain of a ship is more than standing around on deck with your saber dangling between your legs and giving orders. Daniel may be good with a saber, but he knew only a little about running a ship, same as me. Thank you, Father, for all those times you took me to sea.

"Ahoy, cap'n, ship off the starboard bow." The crow's nest sailor was following a new arrival with a brass looking glass. "She's a big one, three masts."

"Coming this way?"

"Can't say for certain. Don't think so, though. Give 'er another minute or two and I'll let ye know."

"Very well. Keep a sharp eye out."

"Aye-aye, cap'n."

"Mister McGinty, prepare a long boat."

"Aye-aye, cap'n. Look alive, mates. Swing 'er over the side."

While McGinty's crew lowered the longboat into the water, I stepped to the rail and looked back to see that Daniel had given the same order to his crew. A smaller boat, but his sailors and mine would be enough for a landing party.

"Mister McGinty, I want you to stay on board."

"Begging yer pardon, cap'n. I'd hoped to be there when ye dug up the treasure."

"I know, and I would have agreed to that, but with the other ship on the horizon I need a man in charge who can defend the ship if necessary. Does anyone else here know how to order the canons to fire?"

"Nay, cap'n. This lot would just point 'em in the general direction and hope the cannon balls fell out of the sky an' down on the ship at the proper moment. There's not an artilleryman in the bunch."

"I'll make sure you get a gold ring with a huge stone in it as a special reward."

We reached the shore and headed for the tree line where the huge rock formation pointed the way to the treasure trail. I counted off the steps we took and tried to remember how far we had traveled on my first visit.

I came to a wide spot in the trail and announced, "Here, dig here."

"Are you sure?" Daniel asked.

"I'm as sure as sure can be," I said and stepped across the trail to the other side where three young saplings stood in front of a large evergreen. "See." I reached for a low limb on the evergreen and lifted my locket from its branch. "I had just enough time to leave this to mark the spot before we moved the boulder."

Huge clouds formed overhead and a few drops of rain fell as the sailors dug deep in the clay and sand. The rain came down lightly and cooled our bodies as the men worked. A breeze filtered through the trees and birds of various sorts battled for rights to sing their songs. I was getting lost in the offerings of nature when I heard a loud clunk as a shovel struck a solid object. The sailors smiled, laughed and cursed,

"Oops, pardon me, cap'n," one of them said.

"Pardon to you, sailor, now get that damned box up here and let's see what we've got."

The crew laughed and Daniel slipped an arm around me and hugged me. A few more scrapings with the shovels and the top of the box appeared. A heavy chest, not very pretty, but apparently quite heavy from the way the men had to muscle it out of the hole in the ground.

"Open it!" someone shouted.

"Nay, let the cap'n open it. 'Tis her right as cap'n."

"Aye, let the cap'n open it."

I stepped forward and levered the sharp point of a pick inside the old lock. I tried, but it was soon apparent to everyone that their captain was still just a wee bit of a girl.

Daniel took the pick from me and snapped the lock open with no effort at all, bringing forth a round of cheers from the crew.

"Open it," he said to me. "I've done the hard work, but you should have the first peek."

All the sailors closed in around the chest as Daniel lifted the lock from its hasp and stood back for me to lift the lid. The next second you would have sworn we had all gone mad. Everyone was diving in and bringing up pearl necklaces, gold chalices and rings and bracelets of gold and silver and studded with rubies, emeralds, all kinds of jewels.

"Stand back!" Daniel shouted. "You're all hoarding the captain's treasure. Put it back."

The men's faces registered their shock, even an angry look here and there, but all of the men did as Daniel had ordered.

Each one dropped their booty back inside the chest. To a man, they did this with nobody holding anything back.

"This treasure is as much yours as it is mine," I said. "First, we get it on board and get back to Portsmouth. I assure you it will be divided equally by buccaneer law."

"Three cheers for Cap'n Esther!" one of the men shouted. "Three cheers for the cap'n," another echoed. "Hip-hip-hooray, hip-hip-hooray, hip-hip, hooray."

The men hoisted the chest on their shoulders, two on each side. We made our way back to the longboats. The silver sands shone brightly in the sun, the waves tossed about in an emerald hue while overhead the sun showered us with a golden glow that reflected off our ships and warmed us as we basked in its rays and in our good fortune.

"Any sign of that ship?" I asked the sailor in the crow's nest.

"It wasn't him, cap'n. I judged 'er to be a merchant ship, seventy ton at best."

"Very good … McGinty, hoist anchor and unfurl those sails. We have a party to attend."

"Aye-aye, cap'n. Ye knows I love a good party."

Sails unfurled, we headed for Portsmouth. Clouds formed and grew dark, which should have been a warning, but I was too happy to heed it.

As we approached the inlet on the eastern side of Lovers' Island, a gunboat took the wind and came abreast of *The Neptune*. The ship flew no colors, which immediately gave us all cause for alarm.

Then, as its canon doors opened, the Spanish flag was hoisted and there for all the world to see was Diego himself, bold as brass, laughing at us.

"You're too late to give fire," he shouted. "My guns are already primed. All I have to do is say the word and your ship will be destroyed."

We flew along at such a speed that we left Daniel and the *Enchanted Princess* behind in our wake.

"Cap'n, ye're not going to give way to this Spanish bastard, are ye?"

"Not on your life, Mister McGinty. Fire the eight pounders."

"The small top deck canons belched a cloud of smoke as their balls whizzed through the air, striking the cabin's quarters and nearly taking Diego's head off his shoulders.

"You down there, don't waste time aiming. Fire the damn canons," McGinty ordered through the open hold.

"Fire!" We could hear Diego order his men.

We scrunched up our shoulders and squinted our eyes in preparation for the broadside we expected to receive from Diego's ship.

Nothing happened.

Not a sound came from his ship.

"Fire!" Diego cursed in Spanish.

Not losing the upper hand, McGinty screamed again at the cannoneers below to open fire. The canons' loud roars came accompanied by columns of blue-black smoke.

"Prepare to board," I yelled.

We grabbed for ropes and were prepared to swing over to Diego's ship when his sails suddenly went slack and *The Neptune* shot forward ahead of the Spaniards.

"He's turning, cap'n," the boatswain announced.

We watched as Diego's ship turned about in the choppy waters.

"Captain Langley," I said.

"D'ye think so, cap'n?"

"Aye, I do. He must have tampered with her fuses. Not a volley did she fire when Diego ordered his men to shoot."

"I'll be buyin' the first pint he drinks next time that we meet."

"And I'll buy the second, Mister McGinty. Take us home."

Chapter 22
The Return Home

"What about your young captain?"

I had forgotten all about the *Emerald Princess*. I need not have worried, however. Daniel sailed close to the island. I suppose he was thinking about going down in the shallow waters if Diego fired upon him. If we were to lose the treasure, best that it be shallow waters instead of Davy Jones' locker. We might recover the whole of it that way.

Diego's ship turned and headed toward the open sea. The man was smart enough to know that the *Emerald Princess* held the treasure, but he was wounded from our guns and knew we would turn about if he fired upon the smaller ship.

A cheer rose from our crew. One of the sailors had a concertina and began playing it. Other sailors started to dance around the deck. They stopped when I walked up to them.

"Play, musician," I said and held my arms out to one of the men. We all danced, and laughed, and had a merry time of it. I danced with every man there except McGinty. I was saving him for last. When I danced back toward him, the crew drifted away and only the sailor with the concertina stayed and played whilst McGinty whirled me around to the music.

The Buccaneer's Daughter

The song ended and the musician set aside his instrument and went back to his duties.

I joined McGinty at the helm and we stood there looking out at the waves breaking gently across the emerald sea. Small white caps dotted the waves. The dark clouds had dissipated and a deep blue sky opened up before us. Sea gulls called out as if to welcome us back from our journey.

We arrived safely from our adventure and loaded with Diego's precious treasure. Father was so pleased when I told him how we fought his enemy. As with every successful journey, we celebrated. I was as drunk as any man and held my liquor better than some of them.

Father turned in early. I gave him a huge emerald ring that fit the middle finger on his right hand. He was pleased with it and kissed me lightly on the forehead.

Tomorrow we would go over the spoils of our capture and divide the treasure amongst the crew after taking our portion, for that is the way with buccaneers. We are one family. We share and share alike.

"I must caution you, daughter. Diego might have been amused before that a mere girl had stolen his ship from him, but stealing his treasure chest is the same as taking food out of his mouth, milk out of his baby's bottle. He has a duty to his men and your actions rob him of the ability to pay them. He will come after you with everything he has. Your very life is in danger and he will not make the same mistake again of underestimating you."

As if I needed any reinforcement of what Father had said, a footman arrived sometime during the night and handed Phillip a letter addressed to me. I opened it, looked at Phillip and he could tell that the note had not brought good news. He knelt at my side and asked to see it. I unfolded the paper and looked to my husband for support. The note read:

Dear Captain Esther,

I extend to you my congratulations on your successful first journey at sea; on the capture of my ship previously and upon the discovery of my treasure chest on Lovers' Island. I hope the contents of which make you very happy and extend your already considerable wealth.

Be so assured that I now have a vested interest in you. I had only a casual interest in your father, although I respect him greatly as a captain and fellow businessman. I see, however, that it is the daughter I should have been watching. I will keep a better eye upon you, my pretty.

I cannot wait until we finally meet in person when I can enjoy your considerable charms in person. After I am finished taking what you have to give, I look forward to plunging my dagger into your heart.

Diego de la Fuentes
Servant to Her Majesty
Isabella, Queen of Spain.

I refolded the letter, noting Phillip's look of apprehension. I had been frightened when I first read the note, now I grew angry at the audacity of the man. If he wanted to fight, I vowed to accommodate him. I had three good ships including his own Man O' War. Together they formed a small armada and, although I had no idea how many ships Diego had now conscripted, I felt we could take the fight to him.

Bravado from a naive young woman? Maybe, but the men had already proved their loyalty to me and their ability to fight like demons. Good men, but Diego held one trump card that I could not beat, he held Captain Langley. He would have concluded by now that we'd had help in escaping his guns, more practical than divine intervention, the physical hand of a friend, and Captain Langley would have been the only soul on board the Spanish captain could not have entirely been convinced of his loyalty. If the young captain were still alive, and I so hoped he was, what would Diego have done with him? There were Spanish seamen in our service who might know the answer. I explained that to Phillip and he agreed they should be questioned.

I sent a runner to McGinty to explain the situation to him.

Chapter 23
The Spanish Sailor

Phillip checked each ship to make sure it held enough provisions for the crew for a month. I insisted on preparing for a long journey. More importantly, he made sure we were heavily loaded with ball and powder for our big guns and an ample supply of the same for our individual arms.

Each man already carried a cutlass or had one below deck, but Phillip added twenty more per ship in case some were lost in battle.

By any standard we were well overstocked, yet nobody objected. It was Father's ships and his money so Phillip, who did not know the sea, and my senior seamen. McGinty and Daniel, said nothing.

Sails and white plaited hemp ropes were in top shape. Word spread quickly amongst the men and I was proud to see them standing tall…and sober. Even the king's navy could not prepare itself better or more admirably than our buccaneers.

As I marched up and down the pier greeting each crew and giving them my blessings and confidence, my spirits were as high as any I'd ever known. The sun was shining, huge billowy clouds filled the sky above, and the squawking of the seagulls all seemed to mesh into a magnificent picture of what the artists call a dazzling array of colors.

Whilst making my rounds, McGinty reported to me with one of the Spaniards he'd questioned. From the Spaniard I learned that Diego worked mostly out of the Cíes Islands, in what is called the Galician Seychelles, which the Spanish government used as a prison. He told us the narrow shoreline ran upwards quite steeply to a levy high up the mountainside. From there, a narrow road led visitors to the mouth of a cave which served as an entrance to an encampment for the guards and the prison entrance beyond that.

"You will lead us ashore?" I asked the Spaniard.

"*Si, Capitan.* I can get you to the guard's camp quickly and silently, but once there you will have to fight your way into the prison."

His name was Jorge Murillo from a well-to-do family. McGinty told me was an outcast and had been forced into service with Diego's fleet. As such, he seemed to hold no allegiance to Diego or to the Spanish government.

"You swear to me your loyalty?" I asked, wanting his assurance.

"*Si.* I am a man without a country. You spared my life and for that I am grateful. I serve you, I will fight for you, and if necessary I will die for you."

McGinty gave me a quick wink to say he believed the man.

"Very well. You will speak to the men going ashore."

Murillo gathered about half the crew and explained the topography of the area and how we would ascend to the mouth of the cave. He would lead the group so as they came into view of the guards he could speak to them in Spanish.

A friendly greeting would allow us to get close enough to draw our swords without causing an alarm.

When Murillo finished speaking he and the others returned to their stations.

Daniel expressed his concern that Murillo might betray us.

"It's a chance we must take," McGinty said.

I agreed.

There seemed no other way to approach the prison except head on. We set sail immediately and headed for the northern tip of Spain with Diego's Man-o-War in the lead flying Diego's own Spanish flag.

The Neptune, the *Enchanted Princess* followed flying no flags. Such action would call for an assumption that they were all together and perhaps the smaller ships were prizes taken in battle.

We weighed anchor in late afternoon in the breakwaters of the Ria de Vigo, one of the deeper inlets that give the Galician coast its serene beauty. These waters linked two of the three islands which make up the Cíes archipelago.

I marvelled at the scenic beauty, watching dark blue waves crash against granite cliffs, sending white spray high into the air. The beach, with its glistening white sand, stretched for a mile north and south, bordered by clumps of dark green pine trees at either end. The sea behind us was rather calm in the deepest part of a jade-coloured bay.

The path from the beach curved uphill, flanked by sycamore, holly and scented acacia. I breathed in the delicate smell of honeysuckle and made my way overboard into one of the long boats we would use for the landing party. The mix of salt and fresh water assailed my senses and I could already taste the fine raw oysters and mussels I knew would be found there by the fishermen.

But we didn't have time to dine. The sun had already set behind us and the vast array of colours faded into shades of grey and black shadows.

This, of course, helped conceal our movements—not an obliteration, but in the lesser light we would be indistinguishable from the few other peasants and sailors scattered about the beach.

We climbed the curved path with Murillo in the lead. He strode with an upright head and perfect posture, the mark of an aristocrat and leader. He could easily be taken for the captain of Diego's ship. He nodded and spoke calmly and assuredly to the people we passed. Pleasantries, I'm sure, but since I spoke no great amount of Spanish I could not be sure of what he said. But nobody gave us any quizzical looks so as cautious as we were, I felt comfortable in him playing his role.

At the top of the trail the cliff spread out a little leading to the mouth of a cave. Three guards busied themselves around a small fire pit boiling crabs in a pot. Two others stood by the entrance to the prison and did not look up as we approached. Murillo spoke quietly to the guards at the fire pit who gave him a nod of friendly greeting.

Daniel and McGinty stepped forward, drew their swords and slashed at the Spaniard's necks.

Huge streams of blood shot forth from both of the men they targeted. As the Spaniards attempted to stand the rest of my crew joined in the slaughter. The attack continued until they fell dead. Murillo engaged the third guard by hand while the rest of the crew charged the remaining two at the cave's entrance. The fight ended quickly, even before I could find a target for my own cutlass. Just as well, I thought. I came to rescue Captain Langley not spend my time in armed battle.

Murillo stood the last guard upright after pummelling him severely with his fists. The man vainly attempted to pull a dagger from the scabbard he wore within a red sash tied around his waist. Murillo was quicker and grasped the dagger from his hand. A quick stab and a twist of the blade in the man's mid-section ended his life. Daniel patted Murillo on the shoulder and held out his hand for the dagger. I stepped forward between them and shook my head. The man had shown his loyalty. I let him keep the weapon and motioned for us to enter the cave. Both men grabbed torches and entered the darkness, with Murillo again leading our little army.

We wasted no time hurrying inside under the light of the two torches.

The Buccaneer's Daughter

Daniel and McGinty fanned out to the left inside the open cavern whilst Murillo and I took to the right. Light from the torches caused the men inside to shield their eyes. It was impossible to tell one man from another. Each prisoner looked drawn and emaciated, their clothes mere rags hanging from their skeletal bodies. Where was our Captain Langley?

"Here, over here, mum." McGinty grabbed a man about the shoulders with his one free arm trying to lift him. One of our sailors rushed to help. The man struggled to his feet under their help, still with bent knees and his head lowered. The scrub on his face bristled in all directions like all the other prisoners, and he stood filthy looking like the others. He reeked of body sweat and other unpleasant smells. But when he lifted his head and I saw the look in his eyes, I knew it to be him. Too weak to offer a smile, showing none of the dashing hero of battle, only a beaten and spiritless soul, but he was alive.

"Take him," I whispered to our men.

"Wait," our prisoner prince beckoned, barely able to whisper his words. "The others...."

McGinty led the way out of the cavern while Daniel directed some of the men to check on the other prisoners. Some of them stood, gaining their inner strength and edging their way slowly towards the mouth of the cave. I didn't want to think of those we might leave behind because they were so close to death they could never survive escaping into the sea. We had no room in the boats but for a few of them.

Our mission had been to rescue our own and we had done that, plus a handful of the other prisoners.

I don't know if all females have a mothering instinct over unfortunates like these men, of if the feeling I had simply came with leadership as a captain responsible for his crew. Her crew in my case. But it was plain that we could not tarry any longer than need be.

We drew many a curious look as we made our way down the hill to the beach. Once again Murillo took the lead and nodded as we passed people along the way. He marched the ragged lot of prisoners in single file with our own marching on the outside as if they were guards.

People looked but never challenged us. I could not believe how easily we moved without incident. That is, until we reached our long boats.

A volley of shots flew into our ranks and two men fell dead, one of them a prisoner and one of our own men.

Our return fire killed one of the Spanish soldiers and another lay wounded. Another soldier still stood but having fired his musket he dropped it rather than try to reload. He ran as two more shots buzzed over his head. He disappeared behind a fishing boat and we hoisted our dead sailor and tossed his body into one of the long boats, leaving the poor retched prisoner behind.

"Murillo, will you sail for me?" He nodded. "Good, take the *Spanish Lady* and follow us. If Diego comes after us, you will have the greater armament and will protect our smaller ships."

The Buccaneer's Daughter

We made our escape and set full sail out of the harbour.

Diego's ship could never catch us until we were on the high seas and even then he could only guess our destination.

We sailed without lights and made a direct run toward Portsmouth. Let the devil himself guide Diego and hope that he takes him straight to hell.

I looked at McGinty as he manned the wheel if *The Neptune*. He was nervous and I supposed it was his fear that I shouldn't have trusted Murillo with our war prize, but I climbed the ropes and looked behind us. The *Spanish Lady* stayed just off our wake with just enough sail to follow us. Murillo was proving a man of his word, laying back to protect us.

We returned safe and sound. Phillip met us at the dock and I flew into his arms, relieved to be home and to be with my husband.

Father arranged for Captain Langley to recuperate in one of the guest rooms. In time, Father would reward him for his tampering with Diego's canons. A ship of his own, or perhaps we would meet Diego again and take another of his ships in battle.

For their services, I promoted Mister McGinty to full captain of *The Neptune* and made sure Daniel stayed on as captain of the schooner.

After so much adventure I only wanted dry land and to assume my chores as Lady Mountbatten.

Sometimes, I still long for the sea. I understand why people say that it gets in your blood. Maybe someday I'll go back to her when I get bored arranging tea parties and banquets for Phillip's business friends.

Maybe someday I will sail a ship again as its captain. After all, I am a buccaneer's daughter, am I not?

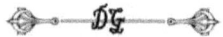

Other Books by Del Garrett

SHADOWLIGHT – Ace reporter Rio Shannon searches for the girl of his dreams in a nightclub called The Silk Rose—a place where a woman can break his heart and government hit men can break his neck. But what's life without a little adventure? *"A well told tale," according to MysteryFiction.net.*

WHILE THE ANGELS SLEPT – When Lydia Taylor's husband dies in an auto accident in Los Angeles, he leaves her so well off she becomes a target for scam artists. Lydia accepts an offer from close friends to stay at their villa in Carmel, but an international gang of art thieves has other plans for her.
Goodreads says, "Del Garrett possesses the fantastic ability to spin a suspenseful tale, full of vivid imagery and a strong attention to the detail surrounding each scene."

TEXAS JUSTICE – An old political enemy sends a killer bounty hunter after a retired Texas Ranger who killed a man in cold blood. The Ranger's adopted son has to track him down before the bounty hunter can find him.

Part I judged as finalist in international eBook competition; Part II won a 1st Place Westward Ho award.

WHISPERS IN THE WIND (THE SEARCH FOR JACK THE RIPPER) – Late night danger lurks for the fallen angels in London's Whitechapel District. Chief Inspector Lionel Diggins. coping with his own personal demons, the death of his wife and his alcoholism, vows to track down the vile killer before Saucy Jack strikes again.

"An intriguing look at the Jack the Ripper murders. Chief Inspector Diggins is a wonderfully noir character. Mr. Garrett does disturbing and icky very well." – Cam Robbins, Novelspot Reviews.

DEL GARRETT'S FLEA MARKET TALES – A collection of his award-winning or previously published short stories, including A Matter of Principal, the Civil War story purchased and published by Louis L'Amour.

"A recommended read," says Shadowlight Review.

THE EL DORADO TRAIL – Kindel eBook – A murderous outlaw kills a storekeeper and steals his money. U.S. Marshal Matthias Lawton rides The El Dorado Trail to bring his man to justice. Trouble is, there's three brothers and only one of him; that is until he gets help from an unlikely source—the cousin of the man who just tried to kill him.

A previously 1st Place winner at the White County Creative Writers conference.

Del Garrett's books are available on Amazon.com. Feel free to leave a review.

For more information about the author, visit his web page:
<u>www.authorsden.com/delgarrett</u>